A DAY IN THE LIFE

T0155045

OTHER WORKS BY SENJI KUROI AVAILABLE
IN ENGLISH TRANSLATION

Life in the Cul-De-Sac

A DAY IN THE LIFE,
AND OTHER STORIES

SENJI KUROI

TRANSLATED BY GILES MURRAY

DALKEY ARCHIVE PRESS
CHAMPAIGN / LONDON / DUBLIN

Originally published in Japanese as *Ichinichi yume no saku*
by Kodansha Ltd., Tokyo, 2006

Copyright © 2006 by Senji Kuroi
Translation copyright © 2013 by Giles Murray
First edition, 2013

Library of Congress Cataloging-in-Publication Data

Kuroi, Senji, 1932-
[Short stories. Selections. English]
A day in the life, and other stories / Senji Kuroi ; translated by Giles
Murray. -- First edition.
pages cm
"Originally published in Japanese as Ichinichi yume no saku by
Kodansha Ltd., Tokyo, 2006"--Title page verso.
ISBN 978-1-56478-865-8 (pbk. : alk. paper)
1. Kuroi, Senji, 1932---Translations into English. I. Murray, Giles,
translator. II. Title.
PL855.U697A2 2013
895.6'35--dc23
2013001668

This book has been selected by the Japanese Literature Publishing Proj-
ect (JLPP), an initiative of the Agency for Cultural Affairs of Japan.

Partially funded by a grant from the Illinois Arts Council,
a state agency

www.dalkeyarchive.com
Cover: design and composition by Mikhail Iliatov
Printed on permanent/durable acid-free paper

CONTENTS

THE THRESHOLD OF DREAMS

It was ten to nine and the sun streaming across the rooftops had only just begun to warm the tips of the camellias by the entrance when he stopped before the heavy-looking wooden door of the Takiguchi Internal Medicine Clinic. The number of commuters hurrying toward the station was tailing off and there was only the occasional distant figure to be seen in the streets of the residential neighborhood. A crisp morning chill lay over the vicinity of the clinic, an old-fashioned wooden building in the European style.

I'm definitely the first person here, he assured himself, but the hand he reached toward the doorknob stopped in mid-air before making its hesitant way back to the pocket of his half-length wool coat. The corner of the pale cream envelope with a cellophane window for the address that he'd been sent by the local city office pricked his finger. It contained the notification about the basic health check that was sent to all local residents over sixty years old, together with his appointment card. Apparently the number of people getting the checkup was increasing every year, attracted by a couple of advantages: the freedom to choose a GP near where they lived and the fact that it cost nothing. The letter recommended making a reservation and going to the clinic in the morning to avoid a crowd.

You were allowed to drink water after getting up, but eating was prohibited; you had to be ready to provide a small sample for the urine test; if you had a cold or otherwise felt unwell, you should inform the doctor in advance and then see whether it was appropriate to have the checkup or not . . . It was very detailed, but he could see that all the points made sense.

The reason why his hand had hesitated briefly before grasping the dully lustrous knob protruding from the heavy-looking wooden door was a handwritten note that had been added in small script with a ballpoint pen beneath the printed instructions: "You must not under any circumstances take the test soon after having strange dreams of the kind you can recall clearly after waking up. This can be harmful."

As it wasn't printed, there was every chance that the message was not part of the standard notice they sent out. Assuming it was a warning that targeted only specific individuals, what kind of people was it directed at? It struck him as odd, given that the checkup wasn't supposed to have any psychological bearing, but he decided not to take it too seriously; as long as he didn't have a dream, everything would be okay.

But he had had a dream last night. It had been a week since he'd made his appointment, and despite having passed a succession of dream-free nights in the interim, of all nights he chose to have a dream on the final one. It was probably closer to morning than night. And to top it all off, it had been unforgettably strange. A dream he did not want to forget.

Taking the handwritten note at face value would have meant skipping the checkup. But the misgivings he felt about the warning being handwritten and the thought of the violent criticism his wife, who had nagged him to make the appointment in the first place, would subject him to if he canceled it, made him decide to ignore it. He could sense, in the twitchy script sloping up to the right, the disagreeableness of some faceless clerk in the Residents' Health and Welfare Division. It was the vexation of some greasy functionary,

10

getting older but unable to find anyone to marry him, that had produced this scribble. Or at least his dream that morning had been interesting enough to set him hypothesizing along these lines.

After getting out of bed, while he washed his face, shaved twice with unusual punctiliousness, and dabbed the eau de cologne his daughter had given him for his birthday on the insides of his wrists, he held on to his dream as though cradling a wet animal wrapped in a blanket to his chest. It only occurred to him he'd probably be better off not putting on this stuff to go to the doctor when the sweet, fruity scent reached his nostrils. Privately, though, he felt the fragrance was in honor of his dream.

Still, he was soon brought back to earth. "You've got to leave good and early and be there waiting when they open the door, or you'll be wasting your time." With this pushy comment from his wife cutting off his retreat and the dawn's dream experience blocking his way forward, he left the house thinking that he'd just have to risk it.

Although it was too late for him to have second thoughts having come this far, the hand with which he opened the door to the clinic still wavered. But he knew that a black sofa and the warm air from a fan heater would be there to welcome the first patient to the empty waiting room . . .

To his surprise, there were three patients already sitting on the sofa, and they all turned at the same time to stare at the intruder who had opened the door. With a muttered greeting, he surveyed the room, avoiding any eye contact. The interior of the old house had been revamped and had a bright look quite out of keeping with the outside. It was so quiet you could hear people breathing, and there was no sign of life from behind the closed reception window. He felt that the not-so-young nurse with the eyes that turned up at the corners had deceived him. "We open the door at five to

11

nine," she'd said when he made his appointment.

There being nowhere else to sit, he ended up standing with his back against the pillar beside the heater, but an old woman slid down the sofa and pointed at the space beside her.

—Have a seat.

Thinking of the time it would take for the three people ahead of him to be dealt with, he nodded his thanks and sat down gingerly on one end of the sofa.

—Have you got the flu? asked the old lady. He had pulled out his handkerchief to blow his nose which had started running as soon as he came into the warmth. She was a fat little person of considerable age with unusually red cheeks and ears that didn't seem quite right for someone of her years.

—No, I've booked a checkup.

—Oh, me too. I don't mind having them if they don't involve anything unpleasant. But I always find coming back to get the results a bit frightening.

—Well, once you've been around for sixty-odd years, it's no surprise that things start going wrong here and there, he replied quietly, his eyes on the two men seated beside her.

—This gentleman here is worried because he had a bad dream last night.

—A dream?

The person the woman had indicated, holding her hand at chest level in a gesture of introduction, was an old man with a round face, almost no hair, and a wool jacket with the zipper pulled all the way up to his chin. His only response to her intrusive comment was an awkward laugh.

—Having a bad dream . . . the test . . . does it . . . ? he asked the man, his upper body straining forward off the sofa.

—Apparently it was an absolutely horrible one, the woman responded before the old man, chewing away on

12

nothing, could reply. His only answer was to slide a pair of hefty palms over his embarrassed face.

—Checkups after a nightmare are never much fun, eh? He addressed the round-faced old man directly, ignoring the woman beside him.

—All topsy-turvy! she said, flapping her wrists as though to drive off something nasty. From her tone he got the impression that she knew what had happened in the other patient's dream, but couldn't bring himself to pry.

—What's more common, positive or negative dreams? The thought in his head popped out of his mouth. Damn it. It was none of his business. He was just unwilling to accept the idea of a photo-negative kind of dream. He could still feel the warmth of the inside of Mrs. Shimane's thighs rubbing against his flanks; she had insisted on being on top.

—All dreams mean their opposite, said the old woman glibly. The old gent at the far end of the sofa, his coat neatly folded on his knee and reading a paperback which he held up in front of his face, cleared his throat. As though it had been triggered by the sound of the heavy phlegm sticking in his throat, his cough continued for a while. On the smoked glass of the reception window a faint shadow could be seen, and it was opened.

—Good morning. Together with the high-pitched voice appeared the face of the almond-eyed nurse, her hair in a red hair band. She looked around the waiting room.

—Mr. Shibata, you're here for a consultation; the rest of you are for checkups.

The old gentleman she had referred to as Shibata nodded through his coughing, while the old woman rose briskly to her feet and walked over to the window, despite not having been called.

—Use this for your urine sample. A little's fine. A teeny bit.

13

Emphasizing her point by pinching a sliver of air between her thumb and index finger, the nurse handed a paper cup to the old lady through the window, then did the same for him and for the round-faced old man. Leaning forward, the old woman bustled off out of the room to the toilet.

After she had left, the two of them sat side by side on the sofa holding their paper cups. The idea that they probably looked as if they were just having a chat over a coffee from a vending machine made him uncomfortable.

—Was there something bad about your dream? he asked, balancing the weightless cup on his knee.

—Yes, yes, answered the other man in a hoarse voice, looking away toward the reception window as if to evade the question.

—But your note didn't say anything about it being better not to get a checkup after having a dream, did it?

Hoping that his jaunty way of speaking would give the impression he was being encouraging, he scrutinized the other man's face with its thin eyebrows.

—I don't think I saw anything like that . . .

The gravity with which he replied only had the effect of making him think that perhaps the man had failed to spot the additional note on his card. His anxiety lingered.

The old woman had shuffled back into the room bearing with great reverence a paper cup which, it was clear even from the sofa, was filled almost to the brim with a liquid swirling from one side to the other. "I rather overdid it," she said apologetically. "No harm done," came the reply from the dismayed nurse at the window.

—You go first. Waggling his paper cup in the direction of the toilet, the old man was murmuring at him, he realized.

—No, no. You're ahead of me.

—I think I'll just see how things play out a while . . .

The way he was holding his hands as if to massage his lower

belly through his thick gray windbreaker seemed designed to suggest that he didn't yet need to go badly enough.

—Well, in that case, excuse me . . .

He got up from the sofa with this brief acknowledgment. The old lady gave a little sigh as she passed him on her way back to the sofa. From the corner of his eye he saw the gentlemanly old fellow, whose name had been called, put his paperback inside his folded coat, give it a pat, and vanish into the consulting room on the opposite side to the toilet.

It was always surprisingly difficult to collect the right amount of pee in the paper cup. Must be even harder for a woman. In no time his dark-colored morning urine had filled the cup half-full and, remembering the space between the nurse's fingertips, he carefully poured some back into the toilet bowl. He wanted to avoid provoking the same disapproval as the old woman had done, but if he misjudged it and threw too much away, the next installment wouldn't come quickly. His hand trembled faintly at the thought.

Turning around after he had passed the paper cup through the little hatch, he found the old lady sitting on the sofa by herself.

—What happened to the fellow who was here just now, the one who'd had the dream? he asked the old woman who had slid down closer to the folded coat.

—He wasn't in the mood so he's gone home.

—Because of the dream?

—Apparently he lost his wife recently.

She continued gazing vacantly in the direction of the window as she answered. Unable to decide if she was talking about the dream or real life, he felt confused. Though he was pleased to move up the list and have a shorter wait, the disappointment at being given the slip was stronger. He couldn't help thinking that the man must have suddenly remembered the extra note written on the form with a ballpoint pen.

15

Losing your wife—he wondered whether that would count as a strange dream.

No longer a busybody, the old lady had shrunk into a tiny, silent presence on the sofa. The ugly pink flower pattern on her cardigan seemed to detach itself from her and force itself on his attention.

—Poor him, he murmured, hoping this could be interpreted either way. Had she heard him? Her expression didn't change. A heavy cough reverberated on the other side of the consulting room door, followed by muffled traces of an exchange.

Maybe I should go home too, came the fleeting thought. It'd probably be better for my health if I went out and had a quick cigarette instead of fretting away in here. An instant later, the weight of the warm paper cup he had just handed the nurse came back to him, and he lost his nerve, as though the cup were a hostage he had handed over. There was something sad in the thought of going and leaving a bit of himself behind.

The door was flung open, and a lanky young man appeared in the waiting room accompanied by a blast of cold air.

—Mr. Yasui, you here for the medicine? asked the nurse, thrusting her head through the reception window.

—No, my throat feels a bit funny. I was hoping the doctor could have a look.

—I see. Will you take your mother's prescription with you?

—I'm going to school after this.

—I see. Is she all right? Not doing anything like eating cat food?

—Not any more. It was just a one-off.

Though taller than the average adult, closer inspection revealed the man to be a boy, with something childish about the area around his eyes and cheeks.

16

—Hey laddie, you can sit down here. As though she'd suddenly woken up, the old lady shoved the neatly folded coat off into the corner and patted the leatherette.

—I'm fine here, replied the youngster as he pulled an exercise book out of the black briefcase he put down on the floor and started to read, his back resting on the wall. The separate personal space he had created was palpable. The silence hung there, no one saying a word, waiting for the door of the consulting room to open. The only sound was the insistent squawking of a crow perched, he supposed, on a nearby telegraph pole.

The old lady gave a start when her name was called, pulled herself to her feet, and slowly moved away from the sofa. The old gent, who came out just as she went in, walked toward the reception window adjusting his cravat. His eyes took in the young man leaning against the wall but soon drifted elsewhere.

The front door opened again and a middle-aged woman appeared with a little girl. She went up to reception and started talking quietly to the nurse, her face half inside the window. Words from their hushed discussion reached his ears in breathy fragments: wooden headrest, slug, toe socks.

He let his head droop and closed his eyes. He wanted to do the same thing as the young man absorbed in his exercise book: to shut out the narrow waiting room and withdraw into his own world. If he could do that, it would soon be his turn for the checkup. Something white started moving in the dim depths of his vision as if it had been waiting in ambush.

It crawled up from behind his eyes to the middle of his head, where it turned into a naked Mrs. Shimane bearing down on his thighs. Lucky I put on my eau de cologne, he thought to himself. Behind Mrs. Shimane were several rolled-up futons wrapped up in a dark green cloth with an

17

arabesque design. Is she about to move house, he wondered.

—No one can see us here, he murmured below the futon bundles. Look. It's honey. Forming a circle with her thumb and index finger, she moved her hand around behind her back.

He knew that would be enough to recharge his batteries. Mrs. Shimane had taken off her glasses and even her face was naked, a face with startlingly soft lips.

Someone was calling his name. He opened his eyes to see the old lady pressing her fingers on the crook of her arm with its rolled-up sleeve as she gave the nurse a courteous bow.

—You're absolutely fine, the nurse told her in a loud voice. No, you don't need anything. Don't forget to come and get the results in a week.

—Right, in a week's time, mumbled the old lady as she made a beeline for the front door. The little girl sat with her trousered legs wide apart in the place occupied until a few minutes earlier by the scrupulously folded coat, while her mother cupped her cheek in her hands, looking stupidly at the engraving on the wall, a view of a temple gate at the top of a stone staircase in the mountains. The young man with the leather briefcase at his feet remained fixed in the same pose staring at his exercise book.

He got up off the sofa and pushed the door of the consulting room open. Dr. Takiguchi, his sturdy build evident beneath his white coat, had his three-page medical record spread across the desk.

—I'm going to take a cardiogram, he announced casually. Please take off your shirt and lie down on the couch.

—Erm . . . is there some kind of rule about it being better not to get a checkup after having a dream? He hadn't planned to ask that question then, but anxiety had got the better of him when he saw the narrow couch with its hard-looking pillow.

—That would depend. What sort of dream did you have?

His scalp gleaming beneath his white hair, the doctor swung around on his rotating chair to face him.

—Oh, just one of those typical, totally unrealistic dreams.

—So you don't want to talk about it?

—Talk about it? Not sure how I should explain it . . .

—Oh, it was one of *those* dreams, was it? The doctor nodded. His expression didn't change.

—I suppose . . . a bit. If you thought there was any danger . . .

—Do you mean inside the dream, or real physical risk?

—I'm worried about both of them.

—Would you stop your checkup if I said it could be harmful?

—That's exactly what I'm trying to ask . . .

Dr. Takiguchi clasped his hands, which had age spots on their backs, put his elbows on the desk, and leaned toward him.

—Your dream or your physical health: which is more important to you?

—Well, my health has held up pretty well this far. But my dream, well, it was the sort of thing I haven't had for years now . . .

—Look, there's little worry that it will affect the results of your checkup. But I can't be sure that my checking your health might not do something adverse to your dreams.

—Adverse? That means . . . ?

—Hmmm. What exactly do I mean . . . ?

Unclasping his interlocking fingers, the doctor shot a glance toward the young nurse standing beside the cardiogram machine.

—Will the dream get broken?

—It might. On the other hand, it could reproduce. The fact

19

that you've woken up doesn't mean that it's dead and gone.

—Reproduce?

—It's up to you, the patient, to decide what to do.

—All right, then. Let's go ahead.

He stood up from his chair and started tugging roughly at his shirt buttons. It was as though the word "harmful" from the handwritten note had started to twitch and glow somewhere on the margins of his dream.

He was concerned that the cardiogram might somehow uncover the shape of his dream, with the naked body of Mrs. Shimane later appearing on his chest X-ray. He wasn't sure what a dream "reproducing" might involve, but he kept telling himself that it was one risk very definitely worth taking.

His blood pressure was just a little high, but neither albumin nor blood were found in his urinalysis, and while there was the suggestion of sucrose, it didn't yet give a plus reaction. The cardiogram revealed that his heart was very slightly tilted over to one side.

—As far as I can tell today, there doesn't seem anything to worry about. Come back in a week to get the more detailed results, said Dr. Takiguchi, his manner dry and businesslike, as he adjusted the angle of a reddish-brown painted wooden doll that stood at the corner of his desk. The narrow eyes of the doll—they could have been laughing or crying—were staring straight at him. Returning its stare, he said thank you and hurried out.

There were more patients waiting to be seen than before and a young man and a fat middle-aged woman were standing leaning against the wall. Surveying the group with a look of pity, he grunted something in the direction of the reception window then pushed the heavy wooden door open.

It was good to be out under the high sky with the cold air stabbing at his cheeks. Sunlight was on the dark green hedges and walls of Oya tuff on one side of the quiet street

20

that he had emerged into.

—Right, he said audibly and paused. He felt that he had completed a task. He put a cigarette in his mouth and lit it. When he started walking it was in the opposite direction to his house.

He was still feeling an unusual physical lightness when he reached the main road and tried to cross it. Going up to the corner where the post office was and waiting for the light was a bore. "As far as I can tell today, there's nothing wrong with you." Dr. Takiguchi's verdict had buoyed him up. The road was separated from the sidewalk by a bed of low azaleas, and with no random pedestrians trying to cross, the cars were passing at quite a clip.

No sooner was there a break in the traffic on one side of the street than a whole series of cars would appear on the other. I go for a walk every day, he thought, my legs are up to it. He pushed through the stiff branches of the azaleas. Every time he looked each way and was about to cross, the speed of the approaching cars made him hang back. Eventually he realized he was hoping for more of a gap than he actually needed. He measured the distance by eye, paused a moment . . . and a car shot past. I should have just crossed. I'd have made it. Angry at his own gutlessness, he craned forward looking for his chance. A boxy car went by on the other side, and he could see a red passenger car behind a refrigerated van on this side. Can I make it? For some reason, it was that moment of doubt that drove him out into the road. A strange pact flashed into his head: if I can get across before it gets here, then my dream will be a positive one. The speed of the oncoming red car was like a swell dragging him in.

—Damn fool!

The squealing brakes, the shouted insult and rush of air merged into a blob that engulfed him. He had crossed the road not in front of the passenger car but right in the path of a

21

small truck that had come scooting up in the opposite lane.

The driver stuck his head out of the window and yelled as he drove by: —At your age, you should cross at the lights. The fucking lights!

Standing rigidly upright on the curb by the azaleas, he raised his hand with a smile of apology. He looked across but the red car had already disappeared. The minute he left the azaleas behind and reached the safety of the sidewalk, the fear hit him in a rush and his knees began to tremble. So it *was* going to be a positive dream, he thought proudly to himself through the trembling. He wanted to give himself a pat on the back: you made it across, not just past the red car, but past a truck that was almost on top of you, so it has to be a positive dream, no doubt about it. The trembling in his legs hadn't stopped but he finally started walking toward the shops.

He was kicking himself for doing something really stupid, but at the same time the elation he felt at having survived the danger showed no sign of subsiding. Maybe it was the excitement that made him come to an uncharacteristic halt in front of a flower shop where rows of pots spilled out into the street. He had spotted a cyclamen, one of the few plants he knew by name, thrusting its flowers up through its layered leaves. The idea came to him on the spur of the moment: I'll buy a potted plant. He quickly settled on a cyclamen with white petals with a reddish-purple tinge at the tips and around the calyx. He chose that one rather than a single-color variety because its flowers somehow reminded him of the pale-skinned Mrs. Shimane. The cherry red that accented the edges of the petals was identical in color to the lipstick she used. When he looked closely, he could even see the same complex of lines as on her lips.

He inspected the shop's modest interior while the shop assistant in her denim apron placed the pot in a plastic bag.

22

There was a poster about the names of flowers beside a tall glass cabinet full of flowers of every color. His curiosity was piqued and he pushed his bifocals high up on his nose so he could better make out the words with his reading lenses. The meaning given for cyclamen was "shy, coy." With a gleeful smile inside, he picked up the surprisingly heavy bag containing the pot and left.

He went into a coffee shop three or four stores further along where he ordered an espresso, placed the pot on the corner of his table, and lit a cigarette. He felt utterly content. Probably because it was still before lunch, there was only one group of men there, apparently discussing business.

—Lovely. Why the flowers?

The young girl who had put his bill on his table was gently running her fingers over the petals that were peeping out of the plastic bag.

—I bought it at the florist's back there.

—Cyclamen. You know what it means?

The unusually outgoing waitress had found the plant's tag among the leaves. She pulled it out and lowered her face to have a look.

—Yes. It means "shy," doesn't it?

Under her influence, his tone was warm and friendly.

—It doesn't say that here.

—Eh?

—It says, Habitat: Mediterranean coast. Family: Primula sieboldii. Also known as: Beacon flower. Meaning: Love's awakening.

—That's absurd. I'm hardly the right age to be buying "Love's awakening."

He pushed up his glasses to check. She was right.

—I just read what it said . . . sorry, there must be some mistake.

The waitress, now suddenly more formal, flitted away to

23

the counter. As if compelled to it by their exchange, he went after her, walking over to the pay phone by the cash register. He unfolded the list of names of his fellow calligraphy students that he always kept in his wallet and rapidly punched in the number for Mrs. Shimane.

—The Shimanes' here. The familiar voice sprang clear and crisp into his ear.

—It's me. We're at calligraphy school together. He could feel his courage ebb away the instant he gave his name. Suffused until now in a happy glow, his name suddenly withered to nothing.

—What can I do for you?

—Nothing—er—in particular . . . just with the weather being so good . . .

—Ah-ha.

—I went out for a walk and bought a potted plant.

—How very nice.

When his opposite number did not even ask what kind of plant, it wasn't disappointment he felt, but consternation. Anxious to bring the call to an end as soon as possible, he couldn't prevent regrettable remarks escaping him like bugs scurrying around.

—Well, actually a number of other things happened before I did that.

—Oh really? What?

—I had a checkup and I almost got run over by a truck.

—Goodness me!

The face on the other end of the line didn't quite match the potted flower after all.

—The flower's a cyclamen.

—They're in season now, aren't they?

Any desire he'd had to tell her about the shape of the flower vanished after her response. The thing now was to stop talking, but he still couldn't figure out how to end the call.

24

—I had a dream this morning.

—You what?

—You must have dreams sometimes, Mrs. Shimane?

—I'm not much of a dreamer.

—Well, I envy you. I'm sure people who don't dream—

—Look, I'm very sorry but I have to go to my daughter's school now. I'm going to be late.

—I'm sorry. I shouldn't have called. Just forget what I said.

She had provided him with the opportunity to end it. He said a flustered good-bye then slowly replaced the receiver, from which she had now vanished. When the waitress carefully brought over his little cup of espresso, he made up his mind to leave the cyclamen there.

He left the coffee shop but had nowhere else to go. On his way home, he crossed the road at the lights, waiting for them to change as he usually did. He had slipped out without saying anything about the cyclamen on the corner of his table, but there was no sign of the waitress coming after him to tell him he'd forgotten it.

—For someone with a reservation, didn't they keep you waiting a long time? his wife, who was watching a cooking program on the TV, turned around and asked.

—There were three people ahead of me, he responded briefly. Since one of them had left, it was really only two, but he couldn't be bothered to go into detail.

—Still, it's faster than the checkups at the hospital I go to. Did they say anything?

—Clean bill of health.

—That you can't be sure of for a week. You need the results of the tests they did.

Paying no attention to what she was saying, he went to wash his hands and gargle carefully. He noticed that his futon was laid out in the middle of the tatami room.

—What's this here for? he asked suspiciously. She was

25

treating him as though he'd just got out of hospital.

—You were the one who told me to leave the futon out. You thought you might want to sleep a bit after getting back from Dr. Takiguchi's.

—I did?

He couldn't remember the morning. The memories were too much of a blur, as if they'd happened a long time ago.

—Looks to me like you need something else tested.

—Perhaps you're right.

He had a sudden sensation of intense fatigue. He removed his clothes and flopped into the cool futon. He was alert and not at all sleepy, but his body seemed to be winding down as if the day were already over. Would he get a better idea of what was going on when he went back to the clinic in seven days' time? He saw the rounded back in the windbreaker pushing the heavy wooden door open as if running away. He saw the old woman in profile looking down, her ears and cheeks so abnormally red, as she crouched on the sofa. The reddish-brown doll was staring fixedly at him with its narrow eyes. Had these things happened today, or were they going to happen in a week's time? He fell into a light sleep before he could work it out.

The corpses of many horses lay on the roof, covering it. Their weight could bring the house down. The horses' heads had slid down and were sticking out above the roof tiles; from the grimacing mouths spewed foam and a liquid that was dripping in a fine thread down from the eaves. Black horses lay heavy and immobile beneath the kitchen sink, beside the table, in front of the refrigerator, their putrid mouths still moist, their faces beaten in. There was no way he could open the refrigerator door.

THE SHADOW HOUSE

A house *is* its exterior. All that people passing by can see is the roof, the walls, and the windows. I'm talking about other people's houses.

Imagine you're in a modest residential area, and the front door of one of the houses in the street is ajar. You can see the corner of the slipper shelf in the doorway, perhaps make out a figure moving behind the lace curtains, but you can't just wander in.

I suspect the affection with which we remember our old homes comes from knowing them from the inside. The way the staircase curved into the landing; the deep blue of a square patch of sky in the kitchen skylight; the flimsy wooden toilet door at the end of the corridor with the stiff bolt—these are the kinds of memories only the inside of a house can provide.

Since the number of houses belonging to other people is overwhelmingly larger than the ones we ourselves have lived in, it seems valid enough to make the general claim that houses consist of their exteriors.

We soon forget about houses we've never been inside. Houses we know only from the outside are nothing more than one piece of the landscape, probably because all they're doing is standing by the side of the road.

I became very conscious of this when construction started on "Mimosa," a coffee shop in an old residential neighborhood nearby. For the life of me, I couldn't recall what the house that had been there before had looked like.

The plot of land it was on had been used as a parking lot for quite a while and there were still places for five or six cars you could rent by the month. To explain it a little better: they had shaved about half the original parking lot off and started building on this, but there must previously have been a house there. Mimosa, in other words, was replacing not a car park, but a house that had been demolished. My memory of it was the one thing I couldn't form a clear picture of.

But before long, things began to fall back into place. A section of a stone wall—it was thick so I guessed it had belonged to a big house—still ran along the road. A shallow box containing a row of earthenware dolls had once been placed on top of this. Their reddish-brown color was darker than normal clay and they looked as though they had been left out in the sun to dry before being fired in a kiln. Oddly flat and crude, the dolls were about the length of my hand. I wondered if they'd been made as wall decorations, since they were too one-dimensional to stand up unsupported. Though not identical, all were of young girls with pigtails, and all had their mouths open. Small though their mouths were, I could feel them shrieking voicelessly inside the box.

These dolls helped me to finally dredge up a memory of a building with dirty mortar walls that had pressed right up against the surrounding wall. I had a hazy image of something jerry-built and shed-like. So that was where the dolls used to live. The realization was a relief. I started feeling more relaxed.

Remembering the house that had gone was a struggle, but I can recall everything about Mimosa from the very first stages of its construction.

Since retiring I had started taking a daily walk, and every time I passed by the site there was always a little old lady standing on the far side of the street watching the building work intently. Maybe "watching" is the wrong word; it was more like keeping the whole thing under surveillance.

Since I used to stop and look at the work being done myself, inevitably we got talking. She told me she lived in the old house opposite the construction site.

—Any idea what kind of building it's going to be?

—From what I hear, it'll be a bit different to everything else around here, she said, staring at the concrete foundation bristling with wooden pillars as if she could see what was coming. Her voice had a slightly bitter edge to it.

—Different?

—Just look at how big that downstairs room is. And I've absolutely no idea where the entrance hall is.

Do wooden buildings really need that many pillars to hold them up? I was so busy wondering about this I didn't have time to pick my way between them and draw out a floor plan in my head.

—No entrance hall?

—I suppose there has to be a way in somewhere.

—A place with no way in wouldn't be much good for whoever had to live there.

—I really don't know what it is they're building. Which was why she was here on lookout duty, her emphatic way of speaking seemed to say. It made me smile.

But as the building work progressed, it became clear that she had a point. Before the exterior walls were put in place, a heavy curved table was installed on one side of the big room downstairs.

—Looks like it's going to be a business of some kind, I said to the old lady, who was leaning against a telegraph pole like a sulky little girl as she observed the building site. Though I couldn't bring myself to say so openly, it was obvious by that stage it was going to be some sort of a bar with a counter. As it was a quiet residential area, her resentment

31

toward an establishment where people would drink seemed reasonable enough.

—Sleaze.

She spat the word out.

—Might be a bother for you living close by.

—If anyone gets drunk and makes trouble, I'll throw a dead cat at 'em.

I was tempted to ask how she would procure this feline corpse, but she looked so angry I was afraid she might knock me down for making a frivolous remark.

—Even if it is a bar, the second floor will probably just be a normal apartment, I tried to reassure her as I looked at the upper section. Since the walls had already been stapled on there was no way of knowing what the interior looked like.

—God only knows what they'll get up to up there. Her tone suggested she could see the whole upstairs with perfect clarity.

—I'm sure it won't be anything improper.

—Oh and I've no doubt you'll be a regular when the place finally opens.

Until then I had felt that we were both street-side observers with much in common. The woman's sudden aspersion came as a shock.

That aside, the suspicion and hatred the old woman bore toward the place that was being built struck me as somewhat abnormal. I sometimes saw her going in and out of her house. It was an old single-story thing hidden behind a hedge with a glass front door with metal slats. Though a small place, unlike most recent homes it had a fair-sized garden, where a few tallish, well-tended trees diffidently spread their branches. If you had lived in a house like this for decades, having a strongly negative reaction to the sudden appearance of a bar on your quiet street seemed understandable enough.

32

She changed the subject abruptly: —Do you remember the house that used to be there?

—Yes, I do. It was where clay dolls were sometimes put out to dry, wasn't it?

—The poor wife . . . such a shame . . .

—Was it she who made the things?

I remembered having seen a middle-aged woman carefully taking a shallow box with dolls in it down from the stone wall when I had passed by on a walk, but I had pretty much forgotten what she looked like. A vague impression of someone rather drab and dull lurked in a corner of my brain.

—I think the dolls she made, they were all crying.

The wrinkled face, all its anger laid bare, was thrust into mine. I had thought the earthen dolls were shouting; it hadn't occurred to me they might be weeping. The small, deep mouths of the figurines, which looked as if they'd been made with the sharp end of a little stick, abruptly came to mind.

—What happened to her?

—Obvious, isn't it? She was thrown out.

—By whom?

—That I don't know. But seeing as this new place is going up after hers was torn down, it's not that hard to guess.

—You were friends?

—She offered me one of her dolls. I couldn't very well say no.

—I wonder what they'd look like if you glazed and fired them?

—No color. No firing. They are what they are.

—Well, they're not really proper dolls then. I thought she might be selling them somewhere.

—She just made the things. All the time.

—What did she do with them all?

—Just kept them. Her house was full of them.

—You actually went in?

—Her place didn't have a proper entrance hall either, but the cement floor by the door, the rooms with Western-style parquet flooring or tatami mats—everywhere from the kitchen to the toilet was dolls, dolls, dolls.

I used to call it the dolls' house because I had seen dolls put outside to dry there. I was taken aback to be told that's what it really was.

—Have you still got the one she gave you?

—It's on my household altar. Next to my husband's mortuary tablet.

—How so?

—Because she's dead. When I first got it, I kept it on top of my chest of drawers, but then after I heard she'd died, well . . . My old man, he always liked young women, so I don't think he'd mind.

That was when I spotted a plumpish man in a T-shirt coming out of the building site. After glancing over at me standing there chatting away to the old lady, he went into something that looked like a windowless telephone box off to one side of the half-built house.

—He's going again. That fellow.

—Eh?

—The toilet. He's got such a weak bladder.

—Maybe he ate something that didn't agree with him.

—No, just you look. He'll be out in no time.

She was quite right. The plump man shut the door of the toilet behind him with a flimsy, hollow sound and hurried back into the house.

—Nothing escapes you, eh?

—Got a lot of free time.

—Once the house is finished, you'll have even more free time. Too much even.

The wonder I felt at her assiduous observation of the

34

place made me want to tease her a little.

—You're always wandering around aimlessly yourself. And as you've got all this time to spend with me, it looks like we're in the same boat.

—Hmm. Well, maybe.

She was right. All I could do was grin sheepishly.

—Got no job?

Here came the second strike. A pensioner, I suddenly felt I'd been demoted to the ranks of the unemployed.

—Well, I've just finished one career, and now I suppose I'm looking for my next job.

—And where do you live?

—Just at the bottom of that hill there.

—In the Hayashida part of town?

—There's a big house with that name on the gatepost nearby, yes.

I pictured the high stone wall around the Hayashida house. They had probably owned much of the area at one time. There was usually a posse of four or five stray cats sitting on their wall.

I was about to ask her how long she had been living on the street when the sound of someone shouting came from the rear of the half-built house. The old woman in her sandals glided over to the mobile toilet, stood on tiptoe, and peered over to where the voice had come from.

—That young fellow's gone and done something stupid again.

She looked back at me, a contented expression on her nodding face, and squeezed her shoulders up against her ears girlishly.

I felt that the construction work on Mimosa had been going on for ages, but in a way it seemed to have gone surprisingly quickly. There were phases in building a house: sometimes progress was obvious, with visible changes to the

35

façade; at other times things seemed to have stalled, it wasn't clear what was going on, and all you could hear were muffled sounds from inside somewhere.

Oddly enough, the closer the place got to being finished, the more things appeared to have ground to a halt. I suppose that though the exterior was finished, the interior decoration work was complicated and took time. Having reached this point, though, the house hardly deserved interested inspection from the road. More and more vans belonging to craftsmen and decorators of all kinds—electricians, plumbers, painters—drew up there, but the appearance of the house itself didn't change a jot.

The one big change was when a sign man attached the letters M-I-M-O-S-A high on the pale blue wall before the scaffolding was taken down. The words "Coffee Shop" were added in smaller letters in front of it.

It turned out to be a coffee shop after all. Not a pub or a bar.

It was in tones of shared relief that I spoke to the old woman when I bumped into her walking to and fro with her hands clasped behind her back looking bored. Assuming she wouldn't disapprove of a coffee shop, I even felt tempted to pop across for a cup of tea sometime.

—I wonder if it's all finished?

Her voice, as she posed the question, sounded gloomier than before. The thought that she'd have no choice but to grin and bear it once the building was finally complete made me feel sorry for her.

—Probably. The scaffolding's been taken down, and it looks like they've finished tidying up around it.

I noticed that the mobile toilet she had pointed out had also gone.

—So when's the place due to open?

—The owner never seems to be around. Have you seen

36

anyone who looks like they might be the owner?

The woman shook her head in silence.

—Could be a while to go yet. I haven't seen any posters or advertising around.

—In the old days they'd have used a *chindonya* band.

I had a fleeting image of a line of *chindonya* musicians, with their white-painted faces and their thick eyeliner, parading around to the sound of the clarinet with sheets of paper saying "Mimosa" stuck to their backs. That might have worked in the shopping streets near the station, but I couldn't picture them in a residential area like this.

—If anyone's going to move in, they're sure to come over and say hello, you being just across the street and all.

—Is someone going to move in?

—Well, the upstairs is designed as an apartment, isn't it? I think it was you who told me that.

—That was something you said. Me, I've no idea.

Unusually, we weren't seeing eye to eye and the conversation was heavy going.

—I have to go.

With a quick bob of her scrawny head and its blur of gray hair, she glided briskly off in her sandals and retreated behind her hedge. From beyond I heard the slatted front door slide shut.

Time passed but Mimosa gave no sign of opening up for business. Though I often walked past, I no longer met up with the old woman.

One evening, I was on my way home after staying out unusually late. Taking my usual route, I turned the usual corner and found myself on the street with Mimosa and the house of the old woman opposite. Mimosa still wasn't open yet, and since no one was living there either, it remained a brand-new deserted house—an odd state of affairs.

Naturally there were no lights on inside, and the pale blue

of the wall facing the street hovered hazily in the light of a far-off street lamp. The night air there felt heavier than elsewhere.

It happened when I was walking along wondering whether there'd be a light on in the house of the old woman, whom I hadn't seen for ages. A little figure suddenly shot out from Mimosa, dashed across the street, and vanished into the hedge on the other side. It only took a moment, like a stray cat crossing the road. I thought I had heard the sound of sandals on the asphalt. When I reached Mimosa, both houses were sunk in silence.

After checking that there was no one following me, I went into the strip of unfenced land where Mimosa stood. The faint light of the distant street lamp just reached the wall that had a window overlooking the parking lot, but the back of the house, which was squeezed up against the neighbors' wall, was quite dark.

Before I had even managed to think of what I would say to anyone who asked me what I was doing there, I had skirted the wall around to the back. I thought I hadn't seen anyone on the street, but could now hear the hard slap of footsteps from over there getting louder by the second. It's so dark that no one will see me if I stay low and close to the wall, I thought as I quickly dropped into a crouch. I then realized I was right beside the back door. My eyes, which had got used to the dark, noticed that there was a thin crack between the door and the wall. Holding my breath until the footsteps went by, I quietly stood up, pulled the door open, and slipped into the house.

The acrid smell of new building materials hit me, and there must have been paper spread on the floor because it rustled under my feet. Taking off my shoes and holding them in my hand, I used the faint glimmer from the window to advance further inside. At the end of a long, narrow room—perhaps the kitchen—was a door which I opened, to be confronted by an empty expanse of floor.

Right next to me was an open space where I imagined the stairs to the second floor would be. I climbed them, treading as quietly as I could and came to a short corridor with several doors. I groped until I found a knob, turned it, and emerged into a south-facing room, probably a living room. This had no furniture either, but there was a single, small, low table plunked in the middle of it. In the light from the parking lot I saw that there was something sitting on the table. It was a flat clay doll.

—So you're up here, are you? I said to it as I picked it up. It was the first time I'd touched one of the dolls, but I knew it was the same as the ones I had seen before. It was hard to make out the expression on its face, but the deep aperture of the mouth was clearly visible.

—So this is your house, eh? I whispered, gently putting the doll, which felt rough on my hand, back on the table. It made a small thunk.

There was a bathroom with a shower, a toilet with a white seat, a kitchen with a bow window, and a Japanese-style room filled with the smell of fresh tatami mats.

I'm in the house. I'm in *someone else's* house. At the thought, a curious sense of satisfaction welled up inside me. I felt almost as though I'd stolen the place.

—Right, I'm off now.

I touched the doll lightly as I said good-bye.

—One day, they'll tear down this house, too. In the meantime, you take it easy.

There was no knowing how long the doll would remain here, and I had no idea myself who would vanish off the face of the earth first, me or Mimosa, but I knew I wouldn't ever forget about this house.

39

I didn't see the old woman again. There was no still no sign of anyone at Mimosa. A few nights later I went to try the back door again, but it was properly locked and wouldn't open. Let's hope that the earthenware doll is still in there, enjoying the quiet life.

EYE

The note from the ophthalmologist told them to be at the clinic at eleven o'clock.

They went into the waiting room, as long and narrow as a railway car, about five minutes early, to find the benches against the walls on either side crammed with nearly twenty people and only a single extra stool still unoccupied.

The consulting and examination rooms were at the opposite end to the door at the entrance, which was latched open. When a patient heard his name being called, he would pass behind a single-leaf screen and disappear inside.

Pointing out the reception desk on the left-hand side to her son, the mother scuttled toward a space on a bench where a woman had just got to her feet. She slid deftly in, sat down, and melted into the atmosphere of the waiting room.

At the reception desk, the son produced his mother's registration card and the appointment note and informed the woman in the white coat that they were there for some pre-operation tests. He explained in a forceful tone that they had come at the time specified by the clinic, unlike the walk-in patients waiting their turn to be seen, but the nurse just nodded gently and indicated a container for registration cards that resembled an empty box of sweets.

It was obviously cramped, but the mother managed to wriggle out of her jacket, which she thrust at her son. Presumably this meant, You look after it. The wind on the walk there had been bracing, cold even, but the waiting room,

43

perhaps because of all the people, was hot and humid.

—Did you tell them that I got a letter and am here for tests? His mother meant to speak quietly, but her voice was distinctly on the loud side. He frowned and nodded without saying anything.

The woman beside her on the bench stood up when her name was called. The mother signaled with her eyes for her son to come over to the vacant seat. Turnover seemed to be surprisingly fast despite all the people waiting, he thought with relief.

Feeling his mother's shoulder poking into his arm, he surveyed the room for a second time.

—It's pretty crowded, he said.

—Did they say anything when you showed them the letter? Her impatient question and his comment passed each other by. He looked annoyed and shook his head. Given the character of the area, you would never imagine that there'd be a place on the second floor of a building around here with—if you included the doctors and nurses—as many as thirty people in it.

The ophthalmology clinic was a neat little building that overlooked a narrow one-way street off the main road. Probably because it was a residential district where numbers of smallish modern condos and older but well-maintained two-story apartments, all with ridiculous foreign names, seemed to be crowding out the rickety wooden houses, there were few people out in the morning streets and an air of calm enveloped them.

A pharmacy and an optician's shared the first floor of the clinic building, but he could hardly remember seeing any customers in either place when his walks took him that way, and he always wondered how they could still be in business.

That so many people were quietly congregating on the second floor of this modest building on its modest piece of

44

land struck the son as bizarre, rather as though a secret society were holding a meeting. And the waiting room wasn't just stuffy, it was charged with a silent current of tension that flowed toward the doctors' rooms at the back.

On the subject of surprises, it was also odd that a building with only three stories should have an elevator. It was a tiny, rattling, boxy thing—an excuse for an elevator really—and he didn't know if it had been installed for people coming in for consultations, or for the inpatients who were apparently upstairs on the third floor.

—Looks like Keiko may be out of luck this time.

The son gave a noncommittal nod, unable to match a face to the name that his mother had suddenly produced.

—Yoshio's been going to see her in the hospital, but they say she can't even recognize her own son anymore.

That second name also meant nothing to him.

—Apparently Michiko didn't bother to go to the hospital at all.

Flinching at the series of names being lobbed at him, he pulled himself upright on the bench and looked over toward the consulting rooms at the back. Irritated, perhaps, at his unresponsiveness, his mother abruptly thrust the black cloth bag that had been on her lap in front of his face. Here, you carry this, was presumably what she meant.

—Quite popular, this place, unlike the shops downstairs, he mumbled, taking the bag with an air of resignation. The thing was soft and squishy and he wondered what could be in it.

His mother, who had been quiet for a while, looked up.

—Don't you think it's probably time to chop down that plum tree?

—Why? Dad always loved that tree.

—Wasn't that my name they called?

An elderly man at the far end of the bench got to his feet

45

and went into the consulting room in response to the name, which was nothing like hers.

He moved his mouth close to her ear. He was starting to worry about how the tests would go and whether she'd be able to talk sensibly to the doctor.

—What's wrong with your hearing aid?

—It's in the bag I gave you.

Perversely, he found her untypically to-the-point response annoying.

—What use is it going to be to you in there? Put it in your ear properly. He hunted for the hearing aid case in the bag she'd passed to him.

—Turn it on then and set the dial between 2 and 3, she said forcefully. Flat and small as a matchbox, the machine emitted a shrill sound in his hand. With his bifocals pushed up onto his forehead, he managed to decipher the tiny numbers and set the dial before placing the flesh-colored earpiece attached to the thin cord in his mother's hand.

She stuck it into her left ear and, after making sure that she had the main part with the switch in her hand, he double-checked that it was working.

—Can you hear me? Is it all right?

—A bit louder. Yes, that's perfect. She nodded contentedly and let her eyes drift around the room while her hand remained pressed to her ear. The spindle-shaped jade on her ring had slipped around to the side of her finger.

—Whenever you go to the doctor you should always make sure you've got it in.

—The old doctor, the father of the present one, comes in on Mondays and Fridays so it's especially crowded then, she explained, ignoring his advice despite probably having heard it.

What was the point? Following her gaze, he too looked around the waiting room. Apart from one mother and

46

daughter, almost all the patients were women past middle age; there were two or three men, but they also seemed to be over retirement age. There was a small woman who was clearly very elderly sitting at the far end of the bench. I bet my mother is older than any of them, he speculated. Mingled feelings of pride and hopelessness churned inside his chest.

She was now older than his father was when he died, she'd told him last year at the seventh anniversary of his father's death, massaging the wrinkled finger with the ring on it. She had celebrated her ninety-first birthday a little while before.

In her remark he had detected something that suggested she felt she'd been in competition with his father and had beaten him. There was also a tinge of what seemed like relief. Why was she making an issue of it? he thought suspiciously, but the self-satisfied tone in her voice lingered all the same.

—I could go anytime now, she'd quickly tacked on in an attempt to cover her true feelings, which she'd let slip out a moment earlier.

Since this mention of "going," his mother had begun to visit the local doctors with even greater regularity than before. She never missed a blood pressure checkup, took a regular cardiogram, went to the dermatological clinic to have a rash treated, and even started a course of injections for osteoporosis. She could walk easily enough without a stick so had the advantage of being able to go to any clinic under her own steam.

—Do you think she'll be all right on her own? his wife used to ask.

—Don't worry. She's the healthiest patient around, he always replied with an ironic smile.

Then recently she announced there was something not quite right about her eyes and went to see an ophthalmologist, who told her she had a cataract and ought to have it operated on.

With her glasses on, she could read newspapers and magazines, and her son, who saw her writing letters and postcards with a fluent hand, had his reservations, but she apparently had made up her mind to have it done after hearing what the doctor had to say.

Since she was of an advanced age, the eye doctor had told her to come in to see him bringing a member of her family with her. He was someone with a good reputation locally, and the son's wife had heard of other old-timers having cataract operations that had turned out well.

An operation was altogether different to just popping into the clinic after a short stroll, and the family would need to know what it was all about in advance. So, having nothing special to do that day, her son had agreed to accompany her on the day of the pre-op tests.

—It's been half an hour so I'm going to give you another dose.

A nurse, who had come out of the consulting room at the back, was addressing the elderly man sitting at the end of the row. She got him to look up, smartly put some eye drops into his eyes, then went off again, her skirt flapping crisply behind her.

That meant that not all the people on the bench were waiting to be seen; some were already undergoing tests and waiting for the drugs to kick in. Tension ebbed from his shoulders at the thought. It was already fifteen minutes since they'd arrived.

—Keiko can't eat anything anymore, announced his mother, suddenly lifting her head from her slumped posture.

—Nowadays they can inject you with drips and nutrients. It isn't such a problem anymore. This not very heartfelt comment was offered for the benefit of an old lady he didn't know from Adam.

48

—Yoshio is past official retirement age and isn't working now. That means he's able to go to the hospital regularly.

—But she doesn't even recognize her own son. He was just repeating what his mother had said earlier. Partly he wanted to check if her hearing aid was working.

—The lad is the same age as you. Or maybe just a little older. Remember how you used to go and play with him, the two of you climbing trees?

A watery sun broke suddenly through the clump of trees to touch the depths of his memory. Maybe that had been the name. Recalling the sensation of the rough bark of the red pine scraping the inside of his thighs below his shorts as he slid down the tree triggered the memory of the subsequent events in the playroom. Keiko must have been the mother with the fine cheekbones and the glossy hair that fell in black waves in front of her ears.

So presumably she'd been talking about that family—the one whose house he'd left in such a horribly miserable state. Gloom closed in on him. There'd been nothing childish about that argument. The other boy's accusations had been withering. Blamed over and over again, he had strenuously denied doing anything wrong—but in the pocket of his shorts his sweaty hand was gripping the fold-up scissors.

He couldn't believe his mother had forgotten about it, since it had culminated in the parents having a brief quarrel. Or had the little episode been shoved away beyond the reach of her decaying memory? He saw the face of the plump child who, he'd been informed, was now past retirement age. It made him uncomfortable. Although he couldn't remember his features in any detail, the memory of his pinkish, sun-burned cheeks and the strange wheezy sound he made when he breathed out came back to him and wouldn't go away.

—Do they still live in Kichijoji? He inquired tentatively, remembering the garden with the pine tree.

49

—They only rented that place. They've been living in an apartment block out in Tanashi for years now.

Clearly the hearing aid was working fine. He was about to add something but thought better of it. Nothing he said was going to stop his mother putting the knife in when she could. He suddenly regretted having made her put in the hearing aid.

—Oh, it's dead. The little girl leaning against her mother's knees as though submerged in a sea of grown-ups gave a sudden shout. Holding a blue ribbon around her neck out to its fullest extent in front of her, she was peering intently at something white and egg-shaped on the end of it.

—Dead again? The mother, a broad woman in a gray sweatshirt, looked down at her daughter with an air of exasperation.

—It was playing happily just a minute ago.

—You probably forgot to feed it.

—No, I didn't. I took really good care of it.

—That's enough now. They always end up dying.

—But I raised it perfectly.

—Mummy doesn't know about that. It was you who were taking care of it. The mother sat back and shifted her gaze to the clock on the wall at the reception desk. There was the sound of the daughter breathing out through her teeth.

He guessed that the egg-shaped toy must be the one that had recently been such a hit that even adults had started getting them, resulting in a shortage which only made it even more popular. He remembered hearing that you had to do all sorts of things to raise a chick, but this was the first time he'd seen the real thing. He found it quite impossible to imagine what the dead chick would look like.

—But I gave it meals, snacks, medicine, love . . . Regret for some irrevocable mistake poured from the child's mouth in a confused monologue unbroken by any pause for breath.

50

There was a hint of theatricality in her voice that suggested she wanted everyone to listen in.

—How are you supposed to bring it back to life? With an affected sigh, the girl presented the squashed white egg with both hands to her mother.

—It's dead. It can't come back to life.

—But you did it before.

—I restarted it from a little chick.

—Do that, then.

—I can't remember how.

At that moment, a boy wearing spectacles with lenses set inside a broad metal frame—the whole contraption looking like a visor with a couple of holes in it—emerged from the back room flapping his hands in front of his chest.

—I can see! I can see! With his face hidden behind the glasses and a pair of chubby thighs showing beneath his shorts, the boy flailed his way over to his mother and sister as if swimming through space. The sister had stood up as though drawn toward him and he sat down in her place, then flapped at his knees, telling her to sit here. Still clasping her white egg, the girl tried to squeeze her thin legs between her mother and her brother.

—They said they'll check me again after fifteen minutes.

—Mummy will come with you to hear what the doctor says.

—What about me? I'll be all alone.

—We won't be long. Feed your chick. Play with it.

—But it's dead. She pouted and let go of the thing at the end of the ribbon so that it dropped onto her chest.

Turning away from this family, he looked at his own mother. Her head was drooping and there was a disgruntled expression on her face as she massaged her shriveled fingers one by one.

It occurred to him that the little girl was probably the

51

youngest person in the waiting room and his mother the oldest. The gap between them could be over eighty years. He was somewhere in the middle, but definitely closer to his mother's side.

—Keeping us waiting like this when we got here at the time they told us to. Honestly! She complained, looking up abruptly.

—They've a lot of people to test. You'll be called any minute now, he told her. As she looked at him, he noticed again that her eyes were gray, like a foreigner's. But they weren't clear; there was a pale, cloudy color covering them.

He didn't know what sort of test she was going to have, but it wasn't likely to be anything too nasty or painful. The memory of the unpleasant duodenal endoscopy he had recently undergone came back to him. Perhaps the only reason he wasn't feeling worried now was that he wasn't the one getting the test.

He hadn't noticed her come in, but a girl in a black jacket was standing by herself leaning against the wall beneath the clock. There was space on the bench near her, but her body language—I'm not like the rest of you—conveyed a desire to keep her distance.

—You have a problem in this part of the vein here. From beyond the screen he could hear the carrying voice of a woman doctor. The patient's mumbled response was inaudible.

—No, no need to worry about that. You don't have any cataracts, which is good in someone your age, and everything else is fine too. So if you . . . The exchange suddenly faded away. Perhaps they had moved and were now facing a different direction.

—It definitely won't be easy. For either of us. From somewhere several seats away came a loud voice that shoved another, less confident voice aside. He couldn't see their faces since they were sitting on the same bench as him, but it

52

sounded like a couple of old women.

—Best thing is to keep your distance. Know what I said to her last time I saw her? Next time I see you will be at my funeral.

The voice had a singsong tone, but alternating resignation and resentment gave it a certain vigor. The rest of their conversation, however, continued in a whisper.

Their name was called. The son jumped to his feet, but his mother, despite her hearing aid, just stared vacantly in the general direction of the reception desk.

—Hey, it's our turn. He tapped her on the shoulder, bony beneath the thin wool garment. The end of the wire, which had fallen out of her ear, was snagged on her stomach.

—You've got to put it in properly if you want to hear what people say to you.

Sticking the tip of the hearing aid into her ear, his mother stood up, wobbled a little, then took hold of his arm.

—This way, please. Only the patient. You will have to wait there. A tall woman in a white coat who had stuck her head around the screen stopped him and pointed to the bench. He noticed an empty seat up at the end nearest the examination room. He supposed it been vacated by a patient who'd just been called in, but nodded and sat down as though it had opened up especially for him.

Settling onto the bench, he discovered that he had a diagonal line of sight into the examination room between the wall and the screen. Two square white boxes that looked like televisions or computers stood side-by-side mounted on stands. From the way the strong voice he'd heard a moment ago—the one he'd assumed belonged to a woman doctor—had reached him, he realized the back part of the clinic was split into an examination room on the right and a consulting room on the left.

The screen prevented him from seeing clearly, but he

53

guessed that someone had told his mother to sit facing the machines. For the time being, the hearing aid seemed to be doing its job properly.

Feeling relieved, he looked at the people on the benches on both sides of the room like someone seated at the front of the train turning around to inspect the other passengers. One of the two women leaning forward intently as they whispered together must have been the lady with the sing-song voice. The girl in the black jacket was almost immobile, like the hands of the clock under which she stood.

Casually turning his attention back to the scene behind the screen, the son was suddenly confronted by a gigantic eye inside one of the boxes. Tilting slightly up to the right, the single eye stared at him unblinkingly, reminding him of a bird of prey. The image being in black and white, and also as expressionless as an inert object, made it all the more unnerving.

He soon figured out that what he was seeing was the eye under examination enlarged to occupy the entire screen of the box-shaped machine closest to him, but he still had trouble conjuring up a human face to go around it. The eye was so still it seemed to be suspended there in isolation.

He guessed it was about thirty centimeters in length. It looked like a hunk of metal and far too heavy to lift even with both hands if you dragged it out of the screen.

The sound of low voices reached his ears. Someone was moving and there was the faint squeaking of a chair. Apparently the patient had moved to the next-door machine while leaving one eye on the other screen. The far rectangle suddenly went white, and an even bigger eye floated to its surface. Tilted diagonally across the screen and with only the vestiges of an eyelash on the lid, it was enlarged and shrunk repeatedly. The instant the adjustments ended, the image again froze on the screen. It was clear that the eye caught on

54

the two side-by-side monitors was the same one.

Surely his mother's eyes weren't that terrifying? He couldn't accept the cold, expressionless image before him as real. The eye on the black and white monitor seemed to have been gouged out; he tried to coax his mother's face from it, adding an eyelid, extending the corner of the eye, adding crow's-feet, sticking on eyelashes. But though he tried hard to remember what her eyes were like, all that floated up were memories from his distant childhood, as if that was where her eyes were really to be found.

Since then, he had seen her dealing with countless different situations and contemplating all kinds of scenery, yet he couldn't recall with any precision what her eyes had looked like at the time. It was almost as though his mother didn't have any. Or only had them up until the day he was born?

If my wife were here, she'd probably have felt completely differently about it. This more considered thought helped him regain his composure.

—Wait here till we call you from the consulting room, said a voice as his mother re-emerged from behind the screen. He was still in a bit of a daze, however. She was missing an eye. She had left it behind in the machine.

After getting to his feet to help her to sit down, he felt compelled to take another look at the examination room. Although they had already served their purpose, the two identical eyes side-by-side on their separate monitors were still there. Perhaps the person in charge of the test had turned the machines off but the images just stayed there, stuck fast to the monitor.

—They're going to call me from this side next time, aren't they? she checked with him, looking up at him with her eyeless face.

—I suppose the doctor has to look at the test results and decide what sort of operation you need.

—Aunt Ikuyo told me her operation only took twenty minutes.

He could detect a note of enthusiasm in his mother's voice, presumably because the test had gone better than she expected. You don't honestly think they're going to operate on you right here and now, do you? He stopped himself expressing the exasperation he felt. If she wanted an operation now it wouldn't be for a cataract, it would involve tidying things up after the removal of her eyeballs and sewing up the cavities.

The boy with the visor and his large mother were called into the examination room. The little girl with the squashed egg dangling from her neck got up off the bench and looked after them nervously. The girl in the black jacket under the clock remained leaning against the wall. The giant eyes on the monitors of the machines he could see between the screen and the wall continued to stare at him unchangingly. No one came to call them into the consulting room.

A SHALLOW RELATIONSHIP

My wife asked me to go to the bank and transfer some money.

I accepted readily enough because there was a branch of the provincial bank that the payee had specified close by; it was actually on the route of my daily walk. The big banks were all in the shopping district near the station, but appropriately enough the provincial bank was unobtrusively located next to a supermarket near an apartment complex on the edge of town. Since I preferred quiet neighborhoods where there were fewer cars, my walk naturally took me that way.

I thought the transfer would be simple to do; the price to be paid for the thing, some food product from another part of Japan, was small, and the branch always seemed to be empty. I almost never saw anyone going in or out.

—No problem. I'll take care of it, I told her. It was only afterwards that I realized that I normally set out on this walk in the evening. Wouldn't the bank be shut any time after three?

—Don't be silly. You can use the ATMs until about seven.

—ATMs? I repeated automatically.

I've withdrawn money by inserting my card and inputting my pin number, but that's a routine transaction. I didn't realize you could use an ATM for sending money even to an unspecified payee.

—The payee isn't unspecified. Because you pay the money into an account at a branch designated by the payee.

—The ATM will do all that, will it?

—Come on, off you go. The machine will tell you exactly what to do.

—Oh, really? was my reaction. I had no idea what I was expected to do.

—You won't make it in the modern world if you can't use an ATM.

With my wife's comment, somewhere between contempt, criticism, and encouragement, ringing in my ears, I set out for my walk with some trepidation.

As my wife had said, there was a cramped space between the metal shutter that closed off the bank's interior and the automatic front doors, with a couple of solid-looking machines up against the back wall. A middle-aged woman with a small, shaggy, black and white dog stood in front of the ATM on the left.

Pretending I knew what I was doing, I strolled over to the machine beside her and peered down at the square screen. "Transfer" was not one of the options listed, but I jabbed a nervous finger at "Direct deposit," guessing that it came to much the same thing. They weren't proper buttons; I had to try and push the words on the screen which was beneath a sheet of thick, transparent material. I didn't trust the whole process. I found it nerve-racking.

The screen changed with a gentle pop.

The next instruction told me to select the first letter of the beneficiary's bank by choosing from a grid of letters. Hastily converting the kanji of the branch name into katakana in my head, I pressed the appropriate letter. All the branches that began with the same letter appeared in two parallel rows on the screen. Oh, I see, the branches in this grid are part of the same bank, so you get away with paying a lower commission.

I nodded to myself as I stood ready for my next instruction.

Having progressed rapidly to the halfway point, the whole procedure ground to a halt at the stage where I had to input my contact telephone number using a keypad. This number is invalid, it said. But that's impossible. I can't have got my own home number wrong!

As I was waggling my head in dismay, the screen jumped inconsiderately back to its original display. I was going to have to repeat all the same steps I'd done already. Maybe I don't need to put in the area code because the bank and our house are in the same district? I omitted it, but got the same result. I repeated all the steps and was rejected. Spurned again.

Feeling thwarted, I looked down at my feet, where my eyes met those of the long-haired dog gazing up at me. Bad luck, old friend, his sympathetic expression seemed to say. No sooner had I started looking deep into his fur-fringed eyes, hoping to find compassion for my plight, than the dog scuttled away, his red leather leash yanked by his female owner, who had completed her transaction.

Outside, it was getting dark. The lights above the machines were blindingly bright. I was worried that I might raise the suspicions of people looking in from the street: what is that man with thinning hair getting up to in that confined space, standing in front of the machine all that time? After all, the guts of the thing were crammed with 10,000-yen notes.

I was about to give up when I noticed a white telephone hanging a little higher up the wall beside the machine. Maybe someone could tell me what to do on this. I had to wait a while.

—Yes, what can I do for you? A man's voice reached my ears. I explained the situation. You did not make any mistakes, so please try again, was all the advice I got. Stifling the urge to say, Look, if you're just on the other side of that metal shutter, why not come out here? I replaced the receiver in the cradle. I repeated all the steps and was rejected again—no change there—but since I was something of an old hand by this stage, the whole process took dramatically less time, even if the result was the same.

There was nothing for it, so I reached for the phone again. But now the line had been diverted to some kind of call center. I didn't know where, but it could be somewhere on the other side of the country.

The next day my wife, who had to go out anyway, returned having completed the transaction with consummate ease.

—Did you use a machine? I inquired.

—Yes I did, she replied.

—That's odd. I cocked my head.

—Very odd, she agreed.

***

I took the subway from Shinjuku.

I was using an SF Metrocard. One of my young friends had told me about them. You can go through the automatic ticket gate directly, bypassing all the hassle of buying a ticket.

I fed the card into the normal slot and was about to go through when the gate closed without much conviction in front of me. What's going on? I had bought the card just a few days ago when the whole limited edition went on sale in the underground shopping mall at Akasaka Mitsuke Station. It featured a portrait of a woman by Matisse from the current exhibition of the Pompidou museum collection.

I was encouraged, though, by the sense of equivocation I'd detected in the way the gate closed. So I pulled the woman and her bulbous shoulders out of the far slot and stuffed her back into the near one. The gates gave way in a slightly

62

confused, hesitant manner.

You're playing with me, I thought as I sauntered through. The woman on the card shrugged her shoulders in apparent agreement. The gate's padded arms started to move lethargically back in, but I ignored the edges, which brushed against my stomach.

I got off the train at Kokkai Gijido-mae Station, but when I tried to use my Matisse lady to go through the automatic gate, the arms blocked my path, this time expressing their refusal in the clearest possible manner. There was none of the playful ambivalence of Shinjuku here; I could feel the firm determination in the way the thing moved. Is this about the different character of the place, I was thinking, when something suddenly clicked. I had bought this commemorative card because I liked the picture, but it was only worth one thousand yen. I had been out riding the subway every day since. Maybe my balance had just run out.

Taking hold of the woman with the heavy shoulders, I retreated sullenly from the gate. A middle-aged man who had come up from behind made a great show of stepping around me before he slipped smoothly through the gate. I felt I had been shown up to be a loser and the problem had nothing to do with money. It was disheartening.

Damn, this is hopeless, I grumbled. I was going to have to stick my card in a fare adjustment machine and see what it said. I looked around but couldn't see one anywhere.

Why? Why? The fractious card scraped against my hand.

All right then, I'll ask. There was nothing else for it, so I gave up on finding a machine and instead walked over to a station employee at an ordinary, crappy old barrier.

The young employee, wearing a round black cap, took the card in his stubby, swollen fingers which went well with a fat, fleshy face. He flipped the woman over after a cursory inspection of her portrait on its sober yellow-brown background.

63

—I got on at Shinjuku, but I can't get through here. There's probably not enough money on it . . .

He subjected the back of the card to another hard stare then fed it into a metal box at about waist level. It seemed to be a know-all sort of machine.

—The problem is, you can't get out here because you didn't get on at Shinjuku.

—That's not true, I protested. I went through the gate properly.

I decided it would probably be better not to tell him that the automatic gate had been a bit cranky with me.

—You really shouldn't have been able to get through, replied the subway man. There was no note of censure or condescension in his brisk voice. He was pointing out a simple matter of fact.

—Are you saying I didn't have enough money left on the card to go through?

—Yes, you were ten yen short.

—I can't understand it. I mean I had no trouble getting in.

A slight sense of anxiety brushed my mind like a faint beam of light: maybe my way of using the turnstile was out of line? But I certainly hadn't forced the thing. It had displayed the tiniest hint of resistance, that's all.

—You shouldn't have got through with this card.

In the clutch of his stubby fingers, the woman trembled slightly.

—I'll pay the difference if I'm short. But I promise you I got on at Shinjuku fair and square. If not, how did I get through the barrier?

The station employee tilted his meaty, florid face slightly to one side.

—Well, you couldn't have done it with this.

I felt a wave of heat inside me; he seemed to be denying the fact that I had caught the train at Shinjuku.

—That's crazy. You don't think I'm lying, do you?

—Look, we're talking about a machine here.

Automatically I braced myself for what he was going to say next: machines don't lie. The blood rushed to my head as I cast around for a counterargument. The employee nudged the brim of his round cap with a finger.

—It's a machine. So it sometimes makes mistakes.

I was caught off-balance by his tone. It was mild, as though he were speaking about a little brother. I took my cue from him and nodded. Why had I never been given too much change from a ticket vending machine? The question had popped into my head unexpectedly, but I stopped myself asking it and groped in my pocket for my purse.

Putting together the balance on my card with the amount I was told I was short, the total seemed to be a bit more than a normal ticket from Shinjuku, but I couldn't be bothered to total it all up and do a double-check. Even the Matisse woman on the card, which had been returned to me, appeared to be shrugging her shoulders.

***

I had to fly from Haneda airport to Hokkaido.

There were only thirty minutes left before the plane was due to take off when I got off the monorail from Hamamatsucho. I definitely wasn't too late, but what with the check-in procedures, the baggage check, and the long corridor to the boarding gate, I didn't have much of a margin.

For some reason I felt more anxious and harried than I normally did when catching a plane.

If I can, I want to get a seat near the front of the plane, I thought as I contemplated the check-in counters stretching out in front of me. There were about ten passengers lined up at any desk with an airline employee.

65

I found a relatively short line and joined it. But there seemed to be a problem of some kind: a little man and woman (I think they were married) were leaning into the counter, and it wasn't going well. The surly-looking lady wasn't making any effort to process the problem pair quickly. In fact, I got the impression she was quite content to accompany the two passengers into deadlock and confusion.

The tall young man standing in front of me tutted in irritation and moved over to the next line. It was longer but you could see that the people in it were being dealt with efficiently. I was tempted, but I assumed that once those two at the front were processed everyone else would go through smoothly, so after counting how many people would be left I decided to place my bet on the shorter line.

Eventually the problem seemed to have been solved. The couple moved over to one side. But the man, apparently unwilling to let things go, turned back and said something to the airline lady. I didn't think he was angry or complaining about anything, just determined to have the last word. The woman responded in kind and the same old tit-for-tat kicked off again.

An angry murmur rose from the people waiting in line as they watched what was going on at the counter. I looked around in a fluster. Surely there was a better way to deal with issues like this?

Our eyes just happened to meet. She was a tall woman standing off to one side in a navy-blue uniform different from the check-in staff, with a round hat on her head, and she was saying something to me. I raised my eyebrows, and with a deferential hand gesture, palm upward, she indicated a boxy-looking machine with a screen. The expression on her face said, I recommend using it.

The woman and the machine stood there so modestly and discreetly that the endless squabble at the counter

66

seemed quite unrelated. Attracted by the peace and quiet they offered, I shuffled toward them.

—Why don't you try this automatic check-in?

I wondered if it really was the same as doing it at the counter. I couldn't understand why no one was using it when there was a queue there that wasn't moving.

—Put your ticket in here, please.

I had no idea how to use the machine, but I felt a sudden burst of optimism: nothing too awful could happen with someone from the airline at hand. The display suddenly changed. There were rows of letters. It was a view of the seating arrangements in the plane from front to back.

—Please select the row you would like to sit in.

Presumably I should press on one of the letters to confirm my choice? I remembered dealing with the ATM in the bank. I'd been all by myself then; now there was someone right next to me.

The next thing was choosing a window or an aisle seat with your finger. I still felt ambivalent about the way the directions were separated from me by a thick pane of glass, but I quickly finished checking in and the machine spat out my boarding pass.

—Is that it? It was anticlimactic, a letdown, and I blurted out the question.

—Yes, that's it. It's very convenient, so I recommend you always use it.

Thanking the face, which was somehow like an offshoot of the navy-blue uniform and the round hat, I looked back at the queue in front of the counter. The couple had vanished and people had moved forward a bit, but there was still a line.

If I had made it to the front and my turn to be served had come around, all I'd have said to the check-in lady would be, "An aisle seat toward the front of the plane, please."

67

What then was the advantage of the check-in staff over the machine? I puzzled over this as I made for the hand baggage security check but no answer was forthcoming.

Extraordinary how when there were so many passengers waiting at the counter, the only person near the machine had been that one employee. Even odder that there had been a woman keeping the machine company like that.

At Chitose Airport on the return leg I found myself having to rethink my ideas at least a little. There was only a handful of passengers lining up at the counter this time, but the memory of my experience at Haneda set my eyes hunting for an automatic check-in machine.

The machine was in use by a middle-aged man in a suit with a leather attaché case. He looked every inch a travel veteran. Operating the device with consummate ease, he completed the process then headed serenely for the boarding gate.

Following his example, I inserted my ticket, but when I tried to select an "aisle" seat at the "front" as I had done at Haneda, the words on the screen were crossed out in red. So there were no empty seats there. What should I do? Though I was getting a bit rattled, I did suddenly notice a "Leave it to us" button. Choosing this might well get me a seat a bit further forward than if I went on and chose "back." With no aisle or window seats free, who knows where I would be put, squashed in between a couple of other people? I wanted to ask and find out but there wasn't anyone near the obviously independent machine. I didn't want to go all the way back to the counter so I caved in and selected "Leave it us."

But how responsive could a machine be?

The upshot of "leaving it to them" was shoehorning myself into the middle seat on a row of three somewhere toward the back. On the window side was a woman of around fifty frantically taking photos of the night sky with a disposable camera. The large man in the aisle seat stretched his legs out in my direction and fell asleep without even waiting for the plane to take off.

Throughout the flight, I couldn't stop thinking that had I communicated my wishes directly to someone at the desk instead of a machine, I'd probably have got something closer to what I wanted. The nasty aftertaste of having "left it" to the machine only begin to wane when we arrived at Haneda and I undid my seatbelt.

***

The organizer of the club of old boys from my old school sent me a note asking me to pay my membership fee through the post office.

The bank was always crowded and I had learned the hard way that ATM transactions there were best left in my wife's hands, so I set off for the post office with a light heart. I knew that at a certain point in the day there was a sort of gap in time when customers just stopped showing up.

I had noticed how, if you waited till a little after midday, there were fewer and fewer customers until by around half past twelve there was almost no one at the counter. Whether you wanted to send an express letter or buy some stamps, there was almost no time-lag between your taking a numbered ticket from the machine on the counter and one of the staff eagerly offering to help.

This was as true of the people who dealt with savings and currency exchange as those who dealt with the mail. Indeed, it wasn't unusual for them to have even fewer customers. I suppose that it was the time when individual customers were busy having lunch and business customers were doing their damnedest not to do any work until they'd got to the end of their lunch break. Elderly customers with nothing to do would take advantage of this lull to drop by and get whatever prosaic little things they wanted done before heading home, mission accomplished. It was a highly satisfactory arrangement for everyone involved.

On that particular day, however, things were a little different from normal. Although there was almost nobody either at the mail window or on the long bench opposite it, I saw three people waiting at the next window along where they handled financial transactions. Worse than that, there was no one behind the window. Maybe he'd gone around to the back to hunt for some documents he needed?

This was turning out all wrong. In frustration, clutching my payment slip, I paced back and forth in front of the counter several times. The clerk still hadn't come back.

There was a more-than-middle-aged woman with glasses seated at the insurance window next door. Looking a little embarrassed about having nothing to do, she turned her puffy face toward me. Apparently none of the customers sitting waiting on the bench went to her window.

Should I just go home, I wondered, with three people in line ahead of me. I mean, I chose this time precisely because I didn't want to waste time waiting for my number to come up. I turned and began to make for the door.

—Is that a money transfer you have there? A faint voice reached me from the other side of the counter. I turned and saw the woman in glasses leaning toward me in her dark green uniform. I was struck by her appearance: she looked like a mother with a son of high school age, not some anonymous post office staffer.

—Where is the person who's meant to be at that window? She looked so friendly that despite myself I asked the question chattily, not in the tone of an aggrieved customer. She said nothing, just stuck out a hand, took the payment form, briskly looked it over, then lowered her voice to a whisper.

70

—With something like this, the machine over there's actually faster.

I liked her voice; it sounded as though she was encouraging me to do something naughty.

—But I'm hopeless with machines . . . Remembering my failure at the bank a few days ago, I wavered.

—It's very easy. Just do what the screen tells you and you'll be fine.

—That's what's supposed to happen, but it never works out that way.

—No. You'll be fine. Go on, try it. I'm not allowed to leave my station otherwise I'd go over there with you.

She talked me through the procedure, moving her hands as though the machine was right in front of her.

—I'm not too confident, but I guess I should give it a go.

—There's nothing to worry about. With the machine, you may even save a bit on the commission.

Her voice, lowered as though to reveal a state secret, propelled me from behind.

I remembered that there was a short passage on the right immediately by the entrance where the machines selling stamps and postcards were. It was only when the woman told me that I realized there was another machine opposite them, its back half-buried in the wall. On its lower belly it said: Automatic Money Transfer Machine. It looked like the ones in the bank, but it was a bit shorter and a little thinner too. It felt more approachable as a result. I guessed that the ones in the bank were multi-purpose machines, while this one was a specialized machine that could get away with being small.

I stared hard at the paper in my hand. It was called a transfer form, I remembered.

I took a couple of deep breaths then solemnly squared up to the machine. I felt the face of the woman who had given

71

me such generous encouragement hovering over me.

It all proceeded more smoothly than expected. My qualms about jabbing my finger at words on the far side of the screen remained, but the machine was happy to do business with me, while I was able to follow its instructions without getting flustered and confused.

The thing was now working away doing some deep analysis down in its belly and I suddenly felt relaxed enough to look back down the corridor. Beside the stamp machine was a door; it was half open, and the dark green jacket of the lady with glasses was protruding through the crack.

—Everything okay? Success? she asked. The voice, which had a faint tremor to it, echoed in the empty passage.

—Yes, thank you. It seems to have been okay.

My voice was louder than I intended.

—I'm sorry I couldn't help you.

—Don't mention it. I'm sorry to have got you worried.

She started to pull the door to and I turned back to the machine. It had produced a little piece of paper labeled "Receipt."

For a moment I felt as though the machine were a nice old neighborhood lady, like the person who'd watched over me through the half-open door. A pleasant delusion.

Carefully placing the receipt in my pocket, I patted the flank of the machine, then decamped.

I wanted to say thank you and report on the final outcome, so I went back to the counter.

—Fast and easy. It's good, isn't it?

The woman with glasses, who still had no customers, gave a little nod and smiled at me maternally.

—Hmm, well . . .

Unable to concur immediately, I cocked my head and smiled back at her. What I was really dithering about, I had no idea.

72

IN THE TRAIN

He couldn't put his finger on when precisely he'd developed his fear of trains.

Calling it "fear" may be going too far, but it was a vague sense of insecurity that made his legs go weak when he was on the station platform, so a word like anxiety would have been understating the case.

Until the train slid into view, he would sit on a bench and look vacantly at the handlebars of the bicycles in the bike racks behind the wire fence, glinting in the sun; look through half-closed eyes at the flowers and leaves on the big white magnolia at the far end, blossoming or dead; smoke a cigarette inside the painted line of the designated smoking area. The conscious enjoyment of an afternoon's outing gave him a warm feeling inside.

He was quite calm when the orange body of the train came into view, looking small far off down the tracks that stretched away in a straight line. He was even happy when the trains appeared on time.

It was when the front section, swaying heavily from side to side, approached the end of the platform at considerable speed that the fear began. He couldn't help thinking that a solid body that shook quite so much was going to hit the edge of the concrete platform, slice it off, and send jagged shards flying everywhere. He simply could not believe that the little gap between the platform and the train as you climbed on board could possibly be enough to deal with the

75

train's lateral sway. Almost unconsciously, he would duck for a moment behind one of the iron pillars on the platform. If the concrete comes flying, I'll probably be okay here, was his spur-of-the-moment reaction.

However, this was like no more than the outermost epidermis of the fear that trains held for him. The real problems started when the train slid safely into the station, slowly came to a stop, and opened its doors along one side. What awaited him inside was a soft, murky something that couldn't be compared to speeding steel or flying concrete. Push it and it would give. Advance and it would recoil. The silent, harmless-seeming atmosphere tempted him to choose coaches with hardly anyone in them, but he found that what should be a comfortable space could have an awful emptiness to it.

Apparently it wasn't the suffocating sense of being shut in with no way out that frightened him. It was the fact that the steel compartment was able to change in uncanny ways, expanding or shrinking almost at will, with people—other members of the species—entering or leaving this habitat.

Why does it all seem so threatening to me? he sometimes wondered.

Casting his mind back, it was clear that trains had been his favorite mode of transport since childhood. On buses he often got sick and vomited out of the window, begging his mother to let him get off in mid-journey. He had no memory of a train ever making him sick.

He had traveled to school by train since primary school, and continued to do so when its name changed to "Citizens' School" with the intensifying war effort, and also when his middle school under the old system became a high school under the new. Going through the ticket barrier swinging his satchel and the celluloid case for his train pass, which was attached to the pocket of his uniform with a length of string, made him feel altogether superior to other students who just walked to their local public school.

He remembered riding the train home with his friends and encountering a local character who had countless badges covering not just his jacket but his hat too, which would set them whispering among themselves and, once they'd made their way further down the aisle, erupting into noisy excitement.

The trains arrived just as naturally as a river flowed; they were a familiar, everyday conveyance that took you to whatever station you wanted to go to after you clambered aboard in your little shoes. Once, though, toward the end of the war, the flow had been interrupted. The train, which had halted in the station when the air raid siren sounded, was strafed by a fighter plane. He had saved himself by charging out onto the platform and flinging himself behind an embankment by the station building. But that very specific fear was different from his present fear of trains.

On one occasion the train in front of the one he was riding had jumped the rails, and they had stopped between two stations, but he managed to jump down onto the grass. The unexpected distance to the ground had scared him, yet that too was a different kind of fear: a purely physical anxiety about hurting his legs when he landed.

One summer a great big hornet had flown in through an open window and a group of high school girls in uniform had all screamed and fled in terror from the furry insect that was buzzing around their heads. But this was another case where it was less about the train than an external thing.

Either way, his memories relating to trains (then called State Railways or National Railways or something of that sort) were fragmentary and episodic. Compared to the dread he felt now, his memories were wholesome, nostalgic, smile-provoking even. In those days he had always felt at home in

77

a train. Anything strange tended to be an intrusion from the outside.

What he felt now was the opposite. It was a horror of the interior when the train had stopped and the doors slid open, saying, "Come on. On you get." It was a loss of nerve about the person he was when he stood waiting on the platform being transformed into a "passenger."

No, not this door, that one's probably better. And he would move along to the next boarding place. But the atmosphere there was worse; it seemed to swell and burst out of the train.

So he would move on, running for the door of a different coach. This one didn't have the hard, spiky feeling of the previous two; instead a waft of odd-smelling breath came from the open, grinning mouth.

Crowding wasn't the reason he found it hard to get on. Confronted with a half-empty car with only a handful of passengers, the open space seemed like a dangerous vacancy in which anything might happen.

Here's no good. I don't like this one, either. As he wavered, the train would get ready to depart. Having to choose one of the doors was a torment.

In time, it dawned on him why. Previously he'd not needed to make choices of this kind.

During his many years of commuting, he always took the morning train at eight twenty A.M., and—at some point it had become a fixed habit—he always used the door at the front of the second last coach. That was how his days began—without the need for doubt or making decisions. Yes, the train was absolutely jam-packed at rush hour, but everyone on board was well-behaved, taking unconscious comfort in the fact they were all traveling as equals, in the grip of wordless resignation.

Even when he left work, the time at which modest office

workers like himself returned home was more or less fixed. If he had a colleague with him, he would just board the train by the same door, then, when the time came, say good-bye and get off. If he were alone, he would be borne along by the human tide and propelled in through some random door, which would then shut behind him.

While ruminating on it, he realized something else. Riding the train had begun to frighten him ever since his life as an office worker had come to an end and he had begun spending more time at home, but the fear wasn't something he felt all the time and everywhere.

Sometimes, when he changed trains en route or hurried home anxious about making it back for dinner, he found himself behaving like a normal passenger. He couldn't recall worrying about selecting a door or feeling any anxiety about what there'd be inside.

In which case, his loss of nerve had to be taking place after he'd left the house and walked to the station, when the train he'd been waiting for on the platform had pulled in, at the very instant that its doors opened. Perhaps the edge of the platform by the tracks represented the borderline between his home life with his wife and going out to places where there were other people?

He encountered other people when he strolled around the neighborhood, but avoiding them was easy. If he spotted someone he knew coming toward him, looking away and waiting until they had gone by was one option, and ducking into a side street was another. If he saw someone in a store, not buying anything was the answer. In the waiting room at the clinic, he could get away with simply crossing his arms and hunching forward until his name was called.

But inside the train was different. Here complete strangers brazenly came and sat down right next to you simply because they happened to be in the same coach. Or they stood in front of you. Was there any other place where people you'd never spoken a word to squeezed up so close to you?

If it all became too distressing and he tried to move elsewhere, pushing his way through the cramped train while it was still moving was clear evidence that he was trying to get away from something and made everyone uncomfortable. The suspicious looks this drew stuck in him like thorns for a long time.

For that matter, some people would stare at him persistently even if he stayed put.

One afternoon, after finally managing to get on board, he sat himself down in a vacant place in the center of a three-seater bench. It looked like a peaceful enough coach; there weren't many people, and apart from what he guessed was a group of high school kids on their way home who were standing and talking loudly, most of the passengers were comfortably settled in their seats.

After sitting down, he made the usual swift survey of his surroundings, checking to see whether anything with the potential to provoke anxiety was lying in wait.

Beside him on his left was an old woman reading a magazine about Buddhism. On the side nearer the door slumped a young man in a suit with a thin attaché case on his knees.

Nearest to the door on the opposite row of seats was a student-looking girl bending forward as she tried to read something on a silver mobile phone; a middle-aged woman clutching a couple of carrier bags with logos on them; and a fat man of around fifty with glasses wearing a navy-blue suit who was sitting with his knees wide apart. He noted how the man's eyes, which were directed at an advertisement for a gossipy magazine suspended from the roof, slid over his face as he settled into the empty seat before quickly going back to the advertisement. He shifted in his seat, trying to find a more comfortable position.

I should be able to make it to my station okay, he thought. He gave a small sigh and shut his eyes. He used to read a newspaper or a magazine even on a crowded train, but he no longer had the patience for small type, and even if he got a seat these days he would always go into defensive mode with his eyes lightly shut. Perhaps because he was so much on the alert, he never managed to doze off, but he got some comfort from the belief that looking asleep by letting his head loll and keeping his eyes shut served as a protective façade.

He wasn't sure how many stations they'd stopped at when the old lady on his left who'd been reading the magazine stood up, leaving the corner seat free. He shifted over into her place.

Looking up for an instant, his eyes met those of the fat man behind his glasses. The man was now directly in front of him. This time his glance did not slide over him. Indeed, he had the distinct sense it had been focused on him for a while already.

It was so intent a look that he almost felt compelled to ask if something was wrong. He was nonplussed for a moment. Had they met before somewhere? The way he sat, taking up so much room with his knees even further apart as if to push the legs of the middle-aged woman with the carrier bags next to him off to one side; the greasy sheen of his complexion; the deep-set eyes behind glasses with thick black frames—no aspect of his appearance made him think this was someone he'd had anything to do with before.

The man quickly turned away and looked out of the window. The train must have been on an elevated stretch of line as all one could see was a cloudy sky, the roofs of buildings, and the tops of some trees. He groped in his pocket, got hold of his handkerchief and wiped the corners of his mouth without needing to, then slumped forward, intending to conceal himself again inside a feigned sleep.

But he had to make one more quick check to see whether the eyes that had been drilling head-on into him had gone or not. If the man had turned his attention elsewhere, then that look, which had a strange glutinousness about it, was just a coincidence and he could probably write the whole thing off as an example of his getting the wrong idea.

There were the eyes. They hadn't moved. They were not threatening or cynical, nor did they contain any hint of mockery; they glowed with a light that seemed to probe inside him.

He thought of the phrase "giving someone the eye." "Eyeballing" was another one. Expressions everyone had used when he'd been at junior high and high school. Apparently they were still in use among the young now. They were about issuing a challenge, and usually meant that an argument or a brawl was just around the corner.

But what was the point of trying to provoke a completely ordinary passenger over sixty years old, who clearly wasn't either well off or physically strong? Even if he had been feeling a bit cranky, he couldn't remember staring back at the other man aggressively. The only possibility was that he might have done something to indicate he was conscious of him. But the first glance they'd exchanged wasn't anything to worry about; worry had only developed in response to that persistent stare.

Unable to ignore the unsettling situation, he tried to think how he could cool things down. As they got closer to the center of town and more passengers got on, there was a chance that someone would come and stand between the sets of facing seats, blocking the man's field of vision. He could then proceed to his destination, get off, and merge into the crowd, bringing the whole episode to an end. After all, whatever happened on the train should end on the train.

But it didn't work out like that. They stopped at plenty of

stations but almost no one got on. Occasionally two or three people would appear, but they sat down in vacant seats, or grabbed hold of a nearby strap and chatted quietly, never coming near the corner seat where he sat. At some point the group of high school children got off, and the middle place beside him on the three-person seat remained empty.

As he wasn't actually asleep, inevitably he opened his eyes from time to time. Pretending he was checking the names of the stations, he would twist his torso around to look out at the platform outside the window. His intention was very much not to look at the other man, but he could feel his gaze sticking to an area from his left cheek down to his chin. The greasy complexion, the fat cheeks, and the glasses with their thick black frames all quivered wetly at the edge of his vision.

Several times he thought about getting off before his stop. But the train had so few passengers, even the smallest movement would be noticed. If he made a dash for the door, that stare, more manic than ever, would follow after him. Who knows, maybe the eyes (and nothing else) would attach themselves to his back and the nape of his neck and come out onto the platform with him. Or just the two of them—eyeball to eyeball—would have a face-off on the edge of an empty platform, with no one else nearby. And even if he managed to escape from him, he had a feeling something worse might well be waiting for him on the next train to come along.

In the end, he stayed put, exposing himself to the stare all the way to his destination.

As the train approached the station, he finally recovered his nerve and got to his feet. He'd made it this far, and he felt a small surge of pride. He would not even so much as look at the other fellow. He had no way of knowing how far the man was going, but he would leave him there, ignoring him completely, possibly even delivering a sarcastic one-liner just before the doors closed behind him.

As he was making his way toward the exit, he was taken aback to see the other man slowly detach himself from his seat. It was almost as if his eyes had hauled the rest of his fat frame upright. Suspecting that he was going to come up to him, he plunged toward the doors and pressed himself up against the glass.

The train slid slowly into the station. A series of pillars displaying the name of the station streamed past, and though he could already make out the features of the people standing beside them, the train still didn't stop. Without needing to turn around, he knew that the other person was standing close enough for him to feel his breath.

Even if the man started something, all he had to do was jump out onto the platform as soon as the doors opened and run for it. He clenched his fists and didn't breathe. He didn't have time to worry about tripping over his own feet and falling over.

At last the doors slowly opened. Just as he was about to step down he felt something warm touch the back of his ear.

—I hope you'll live a long life.

It was more like a blob swaddled in breath than a voice. When he turned to look, he saw the other's thickset back as he went past. The man, who was shorter than he'd imagined, waddled off, rolling his shoulders. He noticed that his suit was not all dark blue as he'd first thought, but had a discreet gray pinstripe.

With the blob of breath still sticking to his ear, he gazed stupidly at the receding figure. To think that he'd stared at him so hard on the train just to say that!

There had been no note of sympathy or encouragement in the voice. He didn't get the impression he was being pitied or taunted either. It had been like the ghost of a sigh,

84

apathetic, resigned, of no more consequence than the sight of a stone on the side of the road.

He couldn't think why he had to live a long life just because somebody hoped he would. Maybe there was something about him that reminded the fellow of his father? The man looked about fifty, meaning his father would be around eighty. He was reluctant to believe he looked quite that old.

One time, he had been standing holding onto a strap gazing vacantly around him when a small child with a satchel on his back who'd been sitting in the special seats for seniors had walked over and tugged at his hand. "Please take my seat," he'd urged. While startled at the child's determination, he was also deflated by the thought, Do I look so feeble to young people? He said thank you, sat himself down, and looked around, but the child had already vanished among the other passengers. What a well brought-up kid, he told himself, to keep his mixed emotions at bay.

But he couldn't help thinking that there had been something a little unnatural in the way the boy had behaved. Maybe good deeds always have something conspicuous about them. Stop over-intellectualizing and just be grateful, he admonished himself, then shut his eyes on the seat he'd been given.

He could remember seeing the exact opposite too.

It was just starting to get dark and there were a lot of passengers standing in the coach. He himself was leaning against a pole which, unsurprisingly, was close to the special seating for seniors in the corner.

A man with receding hair was sitting in the far corner with his elbow on the ledge. Next to the pole and closest to him was the plump, black leather-clad frame of a man of more than middle age. In the middle seat, a young man in a thick jacket, possibly a university student, was asleep with his arms crossed on his chest. Aware that he kept flicking covetous glances their way, he made a conscious effort to stare out of the window into the middle distance.

They pulled into a station somewhere and the majority of the passengers made a move, those leaving switching places with people getting on. The previous equilibrium of the carriage broke down and a new atmosphere pushed its way on board. He was disappointed that no one on the three-seater seniors' bench got off.

There had been a man who elbowed his way through the other passengers toward him. He was a thin, gentlemanly-looking old fellow with a neat side parting to his thinning silver hair, gold-framed glasses, a short white moustache under his nose, and hollow cheeks. His impatient progress through the crowd indicated a stubborn conviction that his way of behaving was right.

Thrusting aside the remaining straphangers, he came to a halt before the seniors' seats. He said nothing, but in a single flowing movement the thin bamboo cane he held in his hand struck the side of one of the knees of the young man sitting in the middle of the row.

The torpid-looking youth with dry, halfheartedly long hair opened his narrow eyes and looked around testily. His expression showed he wasn't quite clear what had happened. Readjusting his crossed arms, he made as if to nod off again. The next blow was a more brisk sideswipe to the top of his knees.

The eyes of the young man looking up met those of the old gent looking down for no more than an instant. He saw the questioning note—What?—in the youngster's eyes. The man with the cane was imperiously gesturing with his chin at the seat he occupied.

The kid finally got the message and rose angrily to his feet after a quick glance at the people sitting on either side of him. What the fuck is going on here? said his sullen expression as he slouched off between the shoulders of the other passengers toward the doors.

The old man quickly settled himself into the vacant space. He sat upright and looked straight ahead expressionlessly. His hands were on the knob of the cane which he held between his legs.

To an onlooker, the episode had something sordid about it. He felt no particular sympathy for the dopey kid, but there was something unforgivably arrogant about the way the old man had made his point with his cane and the tip of his chin. In fact, he hated having had to witness such a scene.

Having someone just stare at you from the seat opposite was obviously preferable to that, particularly when their closing remark, odd though it might be, wished you a long life.

He breathed a small sigh of relief as he walked along the platform to the stairs leading up to the ticket barrier. He glanced casually across to the opposite platform where there was a long row of faces waiting for the train. They would have to ride it. Poor lost souls. Doomed.

Another day, he found himself more worried than usual whether he'd make a success of taking the train back home. The return journey was usually pretty easy, but his sixth sense told him that this might be different. He felt that he was destined to take a train with the worst passengers of his life on board.

That evening the train made an unexpected stop at one of the stations that as an express it would normally have passed straight through. There was an ambulance pulled up by the entrance and paramedics in white helmets ran out onto the platform, with a stretcher.

He lay sprawled on the bench. It was empty, after the passengers who had been sitting beside him had stood up in alarm. The paramedics lifted him up by his feet and shoulders and carried out of the train. His eyes were closed and he didn't move.

—Due to a passenger being taken ill, we have made an emergency stop. We apologize for the inconvenience. We will resume our journey when the problem has been dealt with.

The guard's announcement was broadcast throughout the fretting train.

A couple of minutes later the train slowly began to move.

THE HOUSE NEXT DOOR

It was Monday morning when the doorbell rang. It had been bucketing down when I went to bed the night before, but the rain had miraculously ceased and sunlight was now pouring through the French windows, flooding the living room. My wife had gone to the bank near the station so I was alone. I put the newspaper I'd just started reading down open on the table, and headed resignedly for the front door.

The old Wakamatsus were standing neatly side-by-side on the stone path when I opened the door. They were a slight distance away in a position they could only have assumed by hastily retreating one step after ringing the bell. The house was built on a high foundation, so we always ended up looking down on visitors.

They were both of small build and so unusually dapper that they looked even tinier than they actually were.

—We do apologize for disturbing you when you were probably trying to take it easy, said the skinny wife, with exaggerated emphasis and a bow. "Taking it easy" didn't seem quite the term for the pre-noon period, but I bobbed my head meekly, sensing they knew that I had only been reading the paper. Just because we had been living next door to one another for a long time did not mean that we were particularly close, but the wife would always bow courteously and say hello when I bumped into her in the street.

—We're heading off on something of a jaunt. We just thought we should let you know.

The plump husband had stepped forward a little, almost nudging her aside. The phrase "something of a jaunt" was comically old-fashioned, but I was more intrigued by the way their timing was in perfect sync.

—Oh, a trip. Lucky you. How long will you be gone?

Maybe asking them if they were going abroad would have been the right thing to do. But I didn't. Each of them had a couple of bags, one large, one small, but I could see no sign of a proper suitcase. They looked as though they were about to head straight off to the station. But it wasn't so much that; it was more the sense I got that their "jaunt" was going to be an unglamorous affair.

—Oh, just a week. It was the husband who replied, with a tilt of his high forehead.

—We didn't want you to worry, continued his wife, sliding deftly into his slipstream.

—That's nice of you. I don't know if I can be much use, but I'll certainly be around, so I'll keep an eye on things.

—The house is too old and decrepit to bother about really. We just thought it better to warn you we'd be gone awhile.

—We do apologize for disturbing you, said the wife again by way of bringing the exchange to an end. She thanked me and bowed politely.

—I hope you have an excellent time. Good-bye.

I hastily stepped down from the doorstep to see them properly on their way. They had begun moving off but both came to an abrupt halt, then turned and walked back a few paces. The husband was the first to speak.

—We . . . er . . . rang up to stop the paper being delivered.

—The mail will mostly be just adverts and circulars, so . . . the wife chimed in.

I nodded solemnly and the old couple, looking relieved,

again turned their small backs to me. Off they slowly went down the road, the old man in a thick half-length coat though it was still only early winter, the old woman in a long black coat the hem of which almost dragged along the ground. I felt that the powerful sunlight was pressing them down against the asphalt. I was about to go back indoors when the Wakamatsus' white mailbox with rust at its edges caught my eye. Unnecessarily large and perched awkwardly on the stone wall surrounding their house, it gave the comical impression that it was going to be the one taking care of the empty house.

When my wife returned from the bank, she started grumbling—rather too late—about how low interest rates were. As she replaced her bankbooks and personal seal in the drawers where they belonged, she also complained of the way the man there had treated her.

I waited a moment, then said: —The Wakamatsus next door have gone away.

—Gone away?

The sharply suspicious tone of her question was a residue of her irritation with the bank.

—They've gone off. Both of them.

—So?

—They dropped by to say they were going.

—Why'd they want to do that?

—They'll be gone a week, apparently.

—Really? And where are they going?

—No idea. Didn't ask. The old fellow just said they'd decided go on "a jaunt."

—It's not like them to go away on holiday together.

—You don't think they've done it before?

—As they haven't got any kids, they can hardly be going off to see their grandchildren.

—They said they'd stopped the papers and that we don't

93

need to do anything about the mail as it'd mostly be junk.

—Wonder if they're off for a hot-spring cure?

—Don't think so. They sounded more like a couple of traveling actors.

—And they've left already?

Her expression as she turned toward the next-door house was of someone inspecting something unusual that had only just appeared. The house seemed to me to have suddenly become still and silent.

—And they didn't ask you to do anything for them? Did they give you a key to look after?

—No, nothing like that. I don't think they would ask us. I mean, we don't have much to do with one another normally, do we?

—Well, that's fine then, isn't it?

—Yes. Absolutely.

—So why'd you make such a thing of it?

—They came to say they were leaving. I told you. End of story.

—Thank you kindly for letting me know.

—Glad to be of service.

The conversation ran out of steam and we both were quiet. There was a feeling of unfinished business in the air.

—Right, then, my wife said in an effort to break the mood, and got up and vanished into the kitchen.

I lit a cigarette and picked the paper up again. I read an article on the war in Afghanistan without registering anything. I was looking at a picture of President Bush making a speech when a thought popped into my head: does he have next-door neighbors at the White House? As I leafed through the paper, I wondered idly whether I ought to go and take a look at the outside of the Wakamatsus' empty house.

After finishing my lunch—assorted thick sushi rolls and *inarizushi* with grated-yam soup, which my wife had bought

94

in the shopping arcade in the station building—I shoved my feet into a pair of sandals and sloped off outside. I tried to make it look as though I was out to take advantage of the fabulous weather. Outwardly, my mood was quite calm and casual. But below the surface, as I soaked up the sun's rays, lurked a plan to investigate the uncharted Wakamatsu house. And I wanted to do it without my wife knowing.

The first thing I did was open up our own wooden mailbox, extract a gaudy flier for a takeaway pizza place, and shut it again loudly. I then continued on down the road, sticking close to the walls of the next couple of houses on the way to the station. It was lunchtime in a residential area, so there was almost no one about, just the sun streaming down with lordly abundance. When I looked up at the sky as I shuffled along in my sandaled feet, the sunlight stabbed at my face. Obviously, we had a wonderfully clear sky that day because the rain had rinsed all the dirt out of the atmosphere, but there was still something weird about the weather. Those concepts that the TV and the newspapers liked to feed us —ozone holes, ultraviolet radiation, skin cancer and all that—came to mind and I automatically raised a hand to my forehead to block out the sun.

That's probably far enough, I thought, and retraced my steps. I passed the gate to our place and stopped in front of the Wakamatsus' house. Its appearance hadn't changed since we first moved here: it had been the same single-story building with a tiled roof for over forty years or more. On the side facing the street the hedge that surrounded the property had been replaced by a stone wall after parts of it had withered away, but there was a ragtag bunch of trees growing in the strip of garden around the house. As they were left untrimmed, the building, which was low anyway, appeared to be sunk inside a wood. With the neighboring places both being two stories high, the house, buried under all those

95

wildly growing branches, seemed to be a holdover from a wholly different time.

It was a depressing sight. For some reason there were no trees that flowered or shed their leaves, just the same gloomy green suffocating the place from one year to the next. On the rare occasions I saw the little old husband or wife going in or out, it always made me think of a badger cautiously exiting or returning to its burrow. That was why I had never imagined something like what had happened today taking place: the two of them appearing on our doorstep to announce that they were going on holiday.

On top of the wall with its dirty blotches sat the mailbox, spotted with rust and disproportionately large for a cottage; and immediately beside it stood an incongruously short gatepost. I vaguely remembered that there had been a low metal barred gate back when the wall was built, but that had gone and all that now remained was a break in the wall like a black hole. It was only because the lower branches of the trees stuck out so far that I still got the impression of quite a well-protected house.

As I stood there, I looked in both directions. The street down which the Wakamatsus had gone was so sunny and peaceful, it was hard to believe that anyone could have walked down it after them. I had never felt it before, but now the gap in the wall gaped at me with discreet meaningfulness—to exclude me? To tempt me?

In my sandaled feet I boldly strode into our neighbors' property. I couldn't remember ever having been there before. A tremor of guilt ran up my spine as if I were sneaking in to rob the place. Chilly, damp air hung in the small garden impenetrable to the bright sunlight. I shivered. I was careful, but still brushed against branches dripping with last night's rain. The water ran into my sock and down to my instep.

Right in front of me was a smoked glass door with narrow

96

slats. A small patch of dappled sunlight floated on the opaque glass. I followed the house around to the right, impatient to make a circuit of the place. I guessed that behind the row of cracked wooden shutters, all peeling and ragged at the bottom, was the outer corridor. Beside a small stone slab for putting your shoes on stood a large pot with dried-up grass in it. Beneath the corner of the roof was a heavy-looking indigo charcoal brazier turned upside down and at a crazy angle.

The wooden walls on the side of the house I had gone down were starting to turn white with mold. I hadn't realized that there was a low, pale green wire fence separating this property from the neighbors' and that you could squeeze your way between the wall and the fence, albeit with difficulty. I could see the bright and relatively treeless garden of Mr. Arita, about twice the size of this one.

At the back of the house, parallel to the street, there was a tall precast concrete fence, and I was surprised to find the narrow space littered with broken rice bowls and fragments of plates. Passing below what looked like a small kitchen window, I followed the wall around another corner and was confronted with the side of my house from an unaccustomed angle. A two-story mortared wall loomed up in front of me, and a crack that started below the roof ran to just above the porch. I caught a glimpse of a white figure just outside the front door. The division between our two houses hadn't changed; it was still a holly hedge, desiccated and eaten up by bugs in places.

I stopped. I had the feeling someone was peering at me through the hedge. There was a brief and uncomfortable silence.

—What do you think you're doing in there?

My wife's sharp voice tore through the holly branches. She kept her voice low. It made her anger all the more evident.

97

—Well, er, since they're not here, I thought I'd better give the place the once-over . . .

—Did they ask you to?

—No, they didn't. I'm doing it so I'll be able to tell if anything changes.

I stammered out my responses while trying to escape onto the street, indifferent to the soaking I was getting from the raindrops on the brittle branches of the holly hedge.

—You've got no business doing that. What if someone thought you were a thief?

—Someone? Who?

—Who? The Wakamatsus or the police.

—Well, the Wakamatsus are away and the police don't come around here.

Lunging out into the street with my head down, I found myself confronting my wife over the front gate. Her angry glare made me flinch, yet I still felt pleased with myself for what I'd done.

—What on earth are you up to? You won't do anything around the house even if I ask you, so why are you so keen to stick your nose in their affairs?

—I'm not sticking my nose in. They told me they were going to be away. I was worried . . .

—If you're so worried, then become a security guard. You've nothing else to do here at home.

—But we're not the ones who've gone away.

—Don't talk so loudly about people being away. It's asking for trouble.

—Okay, okay. Look, the weather's lovely. I'm going for a walk.

—Fine. And don't bother to come back.

With this parting shot, my wife headed back inside and slammed the front door behind her. There was something laughable about a couple our age going to the trouble of having an argument outside their own house.

I wouldn't have wanted to stay inside even if she'd told me to. I started ambling in the direction of the station, relishing the weather. She had already been in a pretty foul mood when she got back from the bank and there wasn't much I could do about it. I dragged the heels of my sandals along the asphalt, mulling things over as though to cobble together a defense. As I retraced their route, I wondered vaguely where the Wakamatsus had got to by now . . . and why I had started to think of them as friends all of a sudden.

For a time, our neighbors did not come up again in conversations with my wife. I guess we both felt awkward and avoided mentioning them. Of course, they were difficult to ignore completely since every time we opened or closed our front door their house was across the fence to the left, confronting us. But making a conscious effort never to mention them was tiring and constraining.

At night, for instance, when I was closing the upstairs shutters I'd happen to look down and notice that the area around the Wakamatsus' house—there and nowhere else— was sunk in the deepest darkness. It looked different. There may have been plenty of trees around the house, but I realized that what I usually saw at night was the glow of the light in the porch flickering through the foliage. I couldn't help thinking, if you must leave the house empty, surely leaving the door light on is the very least you can do. While I stared out at the darkness and the emptiness, I had a sudden vision of what the Wakamatsus were doing now. They weren't joggling along on the seats of a bus or train, or luxuriating in an outdoor bath at a hot-spring spa; I saw them from behind, still walking single-mindedly and side-by-side along the road on which they had set off, to somewhere beyond the night.

By the time two days had passed, then three, I had got used to the stillness of the place when I walked past it in

99

the daytime and the silence of it when I looked down on it from upstairs at night. That's what being away is like, I told myself.

It was Thursday, which made it the fourth day, in the evening. I had stepped down into the entranceway to shoot the extra bolt we use only at night when, with a sudden desire to feel the fresh night air, I opened the door a crack and stuck my head out. I also wanted to check the weather as the forecast had said it was going to rain later.

Unlike previous nights, the light was on. An amber glow seeped through the gaps between the thick leaves of the Japanese cypress next to the holly hedge. Without a second thought, I went out into the street and peered through the gap in the wall. The slatted glass door was dimly visible in the light from above.

Are they back? was my first short-lived thought. They had told me they would be away for a week, but there was nothing out of the ordinary about them moving up their dates and coming home early. I stepped into their property to take a better look. The house was pitch dark except for the lantern above the door. While illuminating the garden, its light contrived to incorporate the darkness of the house behind it. Maybe the Wakamatsus had come back that evening and were already in bed. In that case, someone checking out the house late at night would be the object of justified suspicion.

I hurried home, double-locked the door, and called out to my wife who was on her way to the bath, pajamas in hand.

—Hey, the porch light of the Wakamatsus' house is on.

—The Wakamatsus'?

It was her skeptical voice again.

—The place was pitch black last night. I just looked now and the outside light was on.

—Maybe they've come back . . .

100

Oddly, her unexpectedly straightforward manner reminded me that the neighbors' house was supposed to be a taboo subject.

—Since they came by to say they were leaving, wouldn't it be the proper thing for them just to tell us they were back?

—You'd expect that, maybe, but we're talking about the Wakamatsus here . . .

—So they're different?

—Oh, I don't know . . . but what if they're not actually back?

—Then the light came on by itself.

—I could understand if it had turned itself off . . .

—Hmm, yeah.

We fell silent.

—Look, there's no point worrying about it now. You can go and have a look tomorrow.

My wife abruptly stuck out an arm as though pushing something unwelcome away and flicked the bathroom light on with a brisk click. I got a modest satisfaction from knowing that she shared my feelings of uneasiness about the odd goings-on next door.

The light was still on the next day. Though much less noticeable than at night, it was still shining amid the shadows of the trees, merging with the daylight. I knew that there were automatic switches that turned themselves on and off in response to the ambient light, but I couldn't believe that the old couple would have installed anything so sophisticated. And had they done so, it was odd that it didn't turn itself off in the daytime, and baffling that it hadn't turned itself on at all till the night before last.

I waited impatiently for breakfast to end and went out into the street without so much as a glance at the newspaper. I tugged at the slatted door, frowning up at the glow emanating from the dirty white plastic globe that stuck out of the wall. It didn't budge. No surprise there. I pushed the rather cheap and out-of-character bell button but nothing happened. Though I listened hard, I couldn't hear it ringing inside the house.

I went around the side of the house, cooing, "Mr. and Mrs. Wakamatsu?" I wasn't so much calling out to the people who lived there as talking to myself in an attempt to justify what I was doing. Like the last time, I made my circuit going around to the right from the front door; as far as I could tell, nothing had changed.

—Looks like they're not back after all, I said to my wife while she was doing the washing-up.

—How about giving them a ring? she said, still facing the sink, in a tone that suggested she'd been thinking about it for quite a while.

Skimming through the phone book, I found some Wakamatsus on the same street as us from among all the Wakamatsus in the list. I discovered that the old man's first name was Heiji.

I slowly punched the buttons on the phone to contact Heiji Wakamatsu. I was thinking hard, trying to come up with something to say in case he answered.

The ringing went on a long time with no sign of a response. I was about to hang up when the voice of a young woman leaped out of the receiver.

—We are not here to answer your call right now, it said drily. Please call again later.

I put down the receiver thinking that I'd been given a precise, plausible response which I couldn't very well grouse about.

—Apparently they're not here.

My wife turned around. She pressed her fists against her apron.

—You got the answering machine?

102

—I don't know. "Please call again later," it said.

—Well, they're not in then.

—When exactly is "later"?

—A week, or a month, or a year . . .

—You think they'd answer the phone then?

—If they were at home, yes.

There was a hint of something cold, ironic, and barbed in her answer, which was not concern for them.

In the afternoon, my wife went off to the dentist, leaving me feeling as though a heavy weight had been removed from on top of my head. My obsession with the next-door house seemed to be irritating her less now than on the first day, but I was still a little afraid of how she might react. That fear went away when she did, so the atmosphere of the whole house all at once felt free and easy.

I smoked a cigarette, got slowly to my feet, and went out the front door. The sky was heavy with cloud. There was a woman cycling down the street toward me. Pretending to be checking the angle of the TV antenna on the roof until the bike had gone past, I stepped into the next-door property feeling like an old hand. Once inside the stone wall, I felt relaxed enough to examine the contents of the big mailbox. Stuck in the bottom was the garish advert for the pizzeria plus a proposal to get the house's earthquake-readiness checked, a flier from a real estate agent keen to buy up parcels of land, and an ad for a handyman—"I can do any odd job you need." All stuff that I had seen in my own mailbox over the last few days.

Passing beneath the door light with its hazy glimmer like a cloudy eye, I went around to the low stone slab, but the house remained still and silent. I gently tapped the shutters, then, sliding my fingernails into the gaps between them, tried to pull them sideways. They barely moved and I could feel the resistance of the bolts. The pot full of dried-up grass

103

and the upside-down Seto brazier hadn't changed since the last time I'd seen them. At the back of the house I made my way into the narrow passage by the concrete fence. I noticed that the neat little fragments of china that were spread on the ground all had the same pattern, indigo on a white background. Sticking to the wall, I followed the narrow path with its vivid mosaic. The memory was faint, but I thought I remembered hearing from time to time the crack of something hard being struck on the other side of the hedge. I pictured the wife squatting in the narrow gap brandishing a hammer.

My progress came to an abrupt stop as I was passing under the window of the kitchen. At eye level there was a square-shaped meter. A disc like a little CD was slowly revolving beneath a transparent plastic cover. Electricity being consumed in an empty house? I was momentarily startled, but relaxed when I remembered that the front door light was on. The refrigerator was probably humming away in the kitchen too.

I noticed an even sturdier-looking meter a little further along the wall. This one wasn't round either, but had a single horizontal line of movable white numbers on a black background. It didn't take me long to realize it was the gas meter. For no good reason the terms "analog" and "digital" popped into my mind.

I was going to move on when something else caught my eye. Beside the four digits in white was a little box with a series of three red numbers. It was very unobtrusive, but the little red number on the far right was definitely moving up. As I was looking, the "3" disappeared behind the top of the frame to be replaced by a "4."

Not being an expert in gas-related equipment I couldn't be sure, but that had to mean that gas was being used. Elbowing aside any thoughts about gas heaters and gas refrigerators, the fear of a leak invaded my mind. I sniffed the air anxiously, but damp earth was all that I could smell.

My worry that there was somebody in the house and my fear of a gas explosion hovered inside me in a strange kind of balance. I went home feeling unsettled but determined to put a lid on this suspense. I firmly reassured myself that with three days, and then four, having gone by safely, there was no reason for something terrible to suddenly happen now. I looked out of the window; the Wakamatsus' house, quietly hunkered down on the far side of the fence, was exactly the same as it always was.

When my wife came back from the dentist in the early evening I chose not to tell her that next door's gas meter was moving. If I misjudged things, it was all too easy to imagine her making a song and dance about it, calling the gas company and getting them to break into someone else's house. As a good neighbor, that may have been the right thing to do, but I couldn't get rid of the contrary notion that there might be someone inside it. The two ideas were so completely at cross-purposes that plumping for one over the other proved impossible.

Not having told my wife, I casually went out after sunset to buy some cigarettes. There was the Wakamatsus' house with its light on exactly like the night before. I made sure that a man walking two dogs was going away rather than coming toward me, then slipped into the gap in the wall. The red numbers on the gas meter slowly moving upwards appeared in my mind's eye.

I greeted the light in the porch with a slight jerk of the chin. The plan was to demoralize it with a display of mocking condescension. Up above the slatted door the light now seemed to be shining more diffidently than before. Curious, I thought, and moved toward the stone slab. Then my feet froze. There was a whitish glow coming from inside the narrow window above the wooden shutters. Or rather, I only realized there was a long, narrow window up there when I saw how the light was showing. Somewhere inside my head, the digits on the gas meter started spinning faster. A wave of mingled anxiety and relief hit me. Someone was inside, though for some reason I felt it was not the old couple. A thin curtain had been pulled across the window that extended the length of all the shutters, and the shadows of the pleats only served to emphasize the placid nature of the light concealed inside. It didn't suggest an intruder to me; what was seeping out was the tranquility of an ordinary resident.

It was I who was the intruder and, spurred on by guilt, I crept back out onto the street. Forgetting my story about buying cigarettes, I walked along the dark street just to calm myself down. I didn't realize I was going in the opposite direction to the station and the nearby shops. I was afraid that someone else, not my wife, would be waiting for me when I got back home.

Along with the gas meter, the events of that night were something else I didn't tell my wife about. The reason is not completely clear to me, but the baffled sense that something was going on that I couldn't understand seethed inside me. Involving my wife might escalate things. The whole situation could get totally out of hand.

It was Saturday afternoon when the bell rang. I managed to push my way out into the hall just ahead of my wife. The Wakamatsus were supposed to be coming back the next day, but apparently I was already on high alert. Whatever had happened during their absence, I hoped that their return would bring the whole episode to an end.

Standing right in the doorway was a woman of about thirty with her hair pulled back and tied with a thin black ribbon. I sensed she had been looking at the holly hedge until she turned around to face me.

106

—Excuse me. I was wondering . . . are the Wakamatsus away?

She narrowed her eyes behind a pair of rimless glasses. She was looking quite crestfallen.

I spontaneously answered her question with another:
—They're away, are they?

—I've shouted but don't get any response.

—I wonder if they really are away . . .

I wasn't shamming, I'd just let my real feelings slip out.

—The shutters are closed and there are no lights on.

Perhaps she thought I didn't trust her, but she turned to look at the house, her pigtail jiggling behind her.

—You mean the porch light?

—No, I mean the inside of the house. It's dark even in the daytime so they keep the living room light on all the time.

There was something I didn't like in the tone of the woman, who seemed to be even more of an expert on Wakamatsu matters than me.

—Were they expecting you?

—I come here every Saturday. They didn't say anything to me last week.

—Odd, that. They should have warned you if they were going to be out.

Come to think of it, there was something about the woman that made it easy to imagine her briskly tying an apron around her waist and getting down to work.

—I hope everything's all right, she said in a different voice. The pale eyes behind the oval lenses of her rimless glasses opened wide with concern.

—What do you mean, all right?

—Nothing strange has happened, has it?

She spoke with such emphasis I felt as though the responsibility was being laid on my shoulders.

—I'm afraid I've no idea. If you're worried, why not have

a look.

—I already tried shouting and banging on the shutters.

—And?

—As I said, I'm just worried something might have happened . . .

I lurched as someone shoved my shoulder from behind. A face making no effort to conceal its irritation appeared.

—They're not here. They've gone away somewhere, announced my wife beside me in a dismissive tone.

The woman, who had stepped back with a look of surprise, responded with another question. —Both of them?

—Yep. Both of them. Somewhere far away.

—How odd . . .

—We really can't help you. I'm sure they'll be back soon enough. Just you go ahead and do whatever you need to do to put your mind at ease.

With a single haughty nod of her head my wife came down into the entranceway as though to physically drive her off. The woman muttered something, inclined her upper body in a perfunctory bow, and walked away. My wife listened to make sure she'd really gone, then locked the door as noisily as she could.

—Why didn't you just tell her what you know? Why were you stringing her along like that?

—There are some things I don't understand. I thought having a chat with her might help clear them up.

I replied with deliberate calmness to undercut the fervor of my wife, who sent the poor woman packing like some door-to-door salesman.

—Nothing's hard to understand. They left on Monday for a week. That means they'll be back tomorrow.

—Is tomorrow Sunday? Has it already been a week . . . ?

The time felt like a rope paying itself out through my hands. I couldn't tell if it was long or short. Further off I

108

heard a woman's voice shouting, "Mr. Wakamatsu. Mrs. Wakamatsu."

—Did you know that woman was coming to the neighbors every week?

My question was a murmur, more as if were talking to myself. My wife made no reply. As the woman continued shouting, the awareness that the Wakamatsus really were away slowly sank in. I imagined myself in the woman's borrowed glasses, peering at the lifeless, empty house through their lenses.

When tomorrow comes, all this uncertainty will come to an end, I was thinking as I went to bed. The neighbors, who have been away for a week, will come back from wherever it was they went. That was the painfully commonplace ending that unfurled in my mind. The way the woman who'd rung our bell had behaved only reinforced my conviction. But then, remembering the worry in her eyes when she said, "I hope everything's all right," my commonplace ending suddenly started looking shaky; the lights and shadows behind the shutters turned raw and harsh. Maybe they wouldn't come back on the appointed day after all. Maybe this condition of not knowing either way would drag on . . . "Nothing strange has happened, has it?" The woman's insistent voice rose to a shriek that pierced the darkness . . . I imagined the old couple turning up at our front door with a plastic bag full of hot-spring gifts. I also saw myself under the streetlights pacing back and forth in front of a police box before going in to ask what I should do about it.

Managing to ignore my wife's light snoring, at some point I must have nodded off.

There was a loud noise. I woke up with a start. The luminous blue hands of the clock said it was nearly three. The noise seemed to have come from the Wakamatsus' house. The snores beside me had turned into gentle, regular breathing.

109

Quickly I sat upright and groped around until I found my dressing gown, which I dragged over to my side. Now I could clearly hear the shutters around the Wakamatsus' place being thrown open. There was also the faint sound of laughter. Would they really come home at a time like this? No sooner had the doubt arisen than I had thrust my arms into the sleeves of my dressing gown and got up. The floor was cold under my feet. I slipped out of the tatami room where we slept and went down to the front door without turning on any lights.

What confronted me was the sight of a shimmering glow escaping from the next-door house into the clear darkness. As the place was buried in a forest of foliage, such light as managed to break through the gaps was that much sharper, while the brightness inside the house looked capable of projecting the property and the shadows of the surrounding trees far above them.

Shutting the door behind me, I retied the belt of my dressing gown as I went out into the street and peered into the neighbors' house. The slatted door beneath the porch lantern had been removed, and the light that poured over the doorstep revealed shoes swarming there like carp at feeding time. Attracted by the glow from the outer corridor with all the shutters removed, I slipped into the garden and off to the right.

This was the first time I had seen the inside of the house. In it was a throng of old people variously attired in windbreakers and padded kimonos, suits and padded sleeveless kimono jackets, *yukata*s and sweaters, coats and open shirts, baseball caps and long-sleeved undershirts, white aprons and beige long-johns. They were not drinking or singing, just talking away and nodding emphatically and clasping one another's hands and slapping each other's backs as they stood or sat there. They were so boisterous that I caught my breath in surprise. They were all talking, reacting, bursting into laughter at one and the same time so I couldn't make out what anyone was saying. But there were none of the arguments and the shouting you find at a party with young people, and a funny kind of serenity seemed to reign over the interior. The lively scene was suffused with a wonderful radiant energy that streamed off the edges of the house, down into the garden.

I caught a brief glimpse of the profile of Heiji Wakamatsu in his traveling clothes behind a pillar, but quickly lost sight of him as the press of people of similar age and appearance swallowed him. It was as though all their bustle was rotating around a central axis. Not a single one of them so much as glanced in my direction. Neither invited in nor shooed away, I just stood there in shock before this pack of old folks bathed in bright light.

Feeling a gentle tap on my back I turned around. My wife, who had pulled a red shawl over her pajamas, stood there.

—Wow!

That was all I could say.

—Let's go home. It's cold, she whispered.

—Yes, I said, you're right. And I turned my back on the Wakamatsus' house, giving my wife's shoulder a push. Apparently she hadn't turned on the lights in our house. It was drab and hazy in the far fringes of the light seeping from the house next door.

111

MARUNOUCHI

He read in the paper that the first "tree blaster" came after nightfall on November 2. That morning the sun had been out, but he had been surprised how cold the wind, which was blowing straight at him, had felt when he walked over to the local mailbox without a coat. It had gradually died down in the afternoon, and the temperature dropped further as heavy cloud covered the sky.

With the weather being like that, it never crossed his mind that the wind he'd encountered was the first "tree blaster" of the winter. He felt like someone who'd been all tensed up at the thought of an injection from a fat syringe, only for the needle to slip through the skin almost painlessly. There was also a bit of a sneer in there; trees are hardly going to get blasted by that, he felt.

As if to give him his comeuppance, the next day was crisp and clear but also dramatically colder. The wind in question may have been rather feeble but it had left a serious legacy. Its determination to advertise the arrival of winter was loud and clear.

—You'll need a coat.

He was in front of the clothes cupboard choosing a jacket when his wife delivered her warning.

—Oh, I should be fine. The sun's out and I won't be staying out late.

—It's serious winter weather today. We don't want you to catch a cold.

115

He felt her reply was sticking up for yesterday's tree blaster, telling him not to be taken in by its good manners.

—But it's just the beginning of November. A thick jacket will be more than enough.

—It's the temperature, not the date, that I'm talking about.

—This one should be all right, shouldn't it? If I wear a wool shirt underneath.

He showed her the tweed jacket he had dug out from deep inside the cupboard. It was a soft weave, gray herringbone with fine red stripes.

—It's a good piece of clothing, but it's not that warm.

Now that she'd mentioned it, he realized the cloth wasn't as heavy as he'd thought. He liked the texture of the fine wool and the richness of the colors so much that he had worn it with conscious pleasure the last few years. The fact that he'd acquired it at a turning point in his life when he retired from his job of many years, dismissing any qualms about the price in his desire to celebrate his liberation from the tyranny of dark blue suits, may have also been a factor. His affection for it was probably boosted by its being a smart imported brand.

—You're right. The temperature's really dropped off, he mumbled, wanting to justify wearing it and not returning it to the closet. His wife left it at that.

He was only going out to visit his regular optician in central Tokyo to get the results of an eye test and, if necessary, have his lenses updated to match the new prescription. What he wore was hardly important. It would have made more sense to worry about what the lenses were going to cost, but the sunny weather got the better of him and the pleasure of slipping his arms into a favorite jacket after a long interval took precedence.

When he put it on over his dark red shirt it did seem

116

to pinch a bit under the arms, but he didn't tell his wife. Sliding a hand into a side pocket, he pulled out an empty little mothball bag.

—You hardly wore it last winter. It wasn't worth sending it to the cleaner's.

From her voice, he could tell she had just remembered. He could also tell that she'd decided not to make an issue of wearing a coat or the thickness of his jacket.

What really mattered was that this was the first time he'd been out of the house for quite a while. He couldn't remember when the last time was he'd rattled around on the train for an hour or so to go all the way into town. If yesterday's first tree blaster was to be believed, winter had officially begun. Feeling all dressed up for the new season, he stepped lightly up the station stairs. By now he was used to the slight pressure under his arms and it no longer bothered him. He stood on the platform in the sunshine waiting for the town train. It was hard to believe how chilly it had been that morning now. He ran his hands sympathetically over his jacket, free as it was from bulging business card cases or bulky notebooks, and finally put those hands in the side pockets. On the right (the side from which he had extracted the mothballs), his fingers encountered a handkerchief and a purple disposable lighter; on the left a small comb.

One hand, which had now gone inside his jacket, discovered a hard box of cigarettes, then started to probe the front chest pocket by the lapel. On the other side of the fence running parallel to the tracks, the handlebars of the bicycles drawn up in rows glittered in the afternoon sun. There had been a tall tree at the far end before. Despite its position, you couldn't help noticing the clustering white flowers that blossomed on the end of the long, elegantly spread boughs in advance of spring. Most probably a magnolia. It was funny how you hardly noticed the tree's summer or autumn foliage,

117

but in the flowering season it would become suddenly assertive and float up into the foreground. At some point the tree had vanished, either because the bicycle park had been extended or the main road widened. It made sense that he only realized it had gone in the springtime.

As he gazed vacantly at the blue sky where the tree had once stood, the tips of his fingers touched something as they groped around in his chest pocket. It seemed to be a scrap of paper down at the bottom at the furthest extent of his reach. That pocket, he recalled, was surprisingly deep. He remembered how much trouble it had been fishing out things like his medical insurance card or loyalty card which had slipped all the way to the bottom after he had absentmindedly stuffed them in there.

Forced to hurry by the train that came sliding into the platform with its lumbering orange cars, he hooked the piece of paper with a fingernail and plucked it out. It was just a tiny slip of paper like a receipt. Closing his hand around it, he climbed aboard the nearly empty afternoon train, then settled himself in a corner seat and looked around. There was a group of primary school children in short trousers on their way home, enjoying a game that involved singing while waving their hands around at great speed. A young woman and young man seated opposite him both had mobile phones with which they were fiddling. They didn't seem to know one another, which gave a slightly comical look to the almost identical finger movements they were making. The sun that flooded in conspired with the under-seat heating to make the place almost too hot. If he were wearing a coat, he'd probably be sweating.

He leaned back in the seat, slowly crossed his legs in their black wool trousers, and inspected the piece of paper in his hand. It was all quite casual—just having a quick look to see what it was, before screwing it up and chucking it away.

118

It turned out to be a long, thin piece of good quality paper that had been folded in half, actually more like a sheet from a notepad than a receipt. He opened it up and saw something written in black ballpoint ink straddling the crease. It was two sets of four digits linked by a dash. The series of numbers, which had been painstakingly printed rather than scribbled down, was definitely handwritten. He guessed it was a phone number, but he had no idea whose, as there was no name accompanying it. It must have been a number he had taken down and promptly forgotten all about some time ago. Since it had no associations with anything unpleasant, he quickly decided he could ignore the thing. Staring at the four digit dialing code, which could have been for anywhere in Tokyo, he folded the paper in two, then four, bent it into eight and squashed it into sixteen until it was a hard little lump that he bounced up and down on his palm.

It wouldn't do to drop it on the floor and he was about to put it into the side pocket of his jacket when the softness of the fabric stopped his fingers in their tracks. Of course. He must have been wearing it when he took down the number.

But that didn't really lead anywhere. Since he'd been wearing his favorite jacket, though, he would probably have been in a good mood like today when he jotted down the number. He tried hunting out any clues that might be lurking in the back of his mind, but, stymied by the brightness of the afternoon sun, he wasn't able to probe the darkness there very deeply. He was sunk in thought, gazing vacantly at the young woman in the seat opposite, when her face abruptly changed. Stolid, with puffy lips and eyelids, it was now glowing as she contemplated (he supposed) a new message on the screen of the cell phone in her hand. Her smiling face— cheeks puffed out as she tried to conceal her joy from the world around her—revealed a vitality that he wouldn't have suspected in her just a moment ago. As he speculated about

119

what kind of message she'd received, he took out the small, scrunched-up lump of paper from his pocket and carefully pressed it between his hands to smooth out the wrinkles.

I should just call the number and see. At the thought, the sun seemed to shine straight through him. He didn't know whom he'd be talking to, so a certain amount of awkwardness was inevitable, but he could just hang up if things got too uncomfortable. If he used a pay phone, he, as the maker of the call, would be just a nameless voice to the other party. Even if it ended up being a discount electronics shop, a coffee shop, or a massage clinic, just knowing would be enough. As he swayed gently on his seat with the number of passengers increasing around him, the bud of the idea put out branches, developed a thick canopy of leaves, and grew to be an entire tree within the coach.

He got off at Tokyo Station and went down a long escalator where he discovered a bank of gray public phones in a discreet row along the wall of the passageway. Still caught up in a mood of mingled playfulness and a slightly jittery uncertainty, he inserted a telephone card he had pulled out of his wallet and dialed the number on the creased scrap of paper. There was a brief pause, then he heard the sound of ringing in the receiver.

He held his breath and counted five rings before the mumbly voice of a woman emerged on the other end of the line.

—Hello? was all she said. She must have been somewhere quiet as there was no background noise at all. The least she could do was say her name. Disappointed, he felt the hard, barren silence pressing on him. She gave no sign of hanging up, which only made him more flustered.

—Oh, hello. I . . . erm . . .

—You finally decided to get in touch. Where are you calling from?

120

—I just got off the train at Tokyo Station.

Flummoxed by the way the conversation was developing, he could only offer the most banal of responses. For a moment he had the illusion that he'd left the house specifically to make this call.

—You know the new Maru Building that just opened? That's where I'm going.

She thinks I'm someone else. A new wave of dismay swept over him. He'd never heard the voice before.

—Erm, but I . . .

—Yes, I know. What have you got to do now?

—I'm going to an optician on the Yaesu side of the station.

—That's perfect. I can be at the Maru Building in under half an hour.

—But I'm not planning to go to the Maru Building.

—Be careful; it's not the New Maru Building, it's the new old Maru Building. It's just been rebuilt. It's around thirty stories high now.

—I heard about the rebuilding, but I wasn't planning to . . .

—Was it the fourth floor? No, the fifth, I think. There's a terrace overlooking the station you can go out on. It'll be nice, though it may be a bit chilly.

—And why exactly will I be going there?

He was annoyed at being forced to do whatever this woman wanted, and spontaneously his tone turned nasty. The other voice vanished from the receiver immediately. At first he thought she'd just gone quiet, but when his repeated hellos elicited no reply, he started worrying that she had given up and walked away. If it all ended here, he'd be left with the sour taste of total incomprehension. But if she hadn't hung up, then his only option was to be equally obstinate and wait her out.

The telephone card, which was a ritual gift he'd been given

121

together with a thin bag of salt at the funeral of a friend, was running through its remaining credits silently. Will I have to wait till I'm down to zero? He was shifting his weight from foot to foot when something more like a faint current of air than an articulate sound floated by his ear. From within it a low voice stripped of anything demanding reached his eardrum. It was so quiet that she seemed to be at a greater distance from him than before.

—Why did you call me?

—Because . . . he started to reply, but was at a loss for words. What sort of explanation could he give when he didn't even know whom he was talking to?

—It's just a game for you. A whim . . .

The quiet, knowing voice flowed out of the receiver.

—That's not true. It wasn't easy for me to make this call.

—You're just killing time before going to the optician's . . . Or were you planning to say good-bye and good riddance?

—You're wrong. I just wanted to find out.

I'm not lying to her, he thought with a certain desperation. He hunted deep inside himself for the memory of even a vaguely similar voice, but came up with nothing. One thing he knew was that there was a weight, heavy and immovable, inside his chest.

—You just do whatever you want.

The tone was dismissive. There was a pause and the phone was cut off. He felt as if he had been suddenly shoved back out into the passageway at the foot of the escalator with all the people milling to and fro and forced to stand there naked. A man came toward him pushing a big suitcase on rumbling wheels. A couple of businessmen clutching brief-cases and conferring in low voices hurried past him. An old woman trotted along behind a girl in a white woolen hat. A very erect woman with the collar of her red coat turned

122

up was walking toward the main passage, her boots leaving echoing footsteps in her wake. It was all so bright and lively. He felt out of place, as though he had just crawled out from the dark corner of some warehouse.

He stood there dumbly for a while, but in the end heading for the optician's was the only thing to do. He checked his watch before setting off. He was interested in having a proper look at the tall new Maru Building since he hadn't yet done so, but would obviously need to leave the station through the gate on the Marunouchi side for that. Giving up on the idea, he followed the passageway to the Yaesu exit on the opposite side. He felt a tinge of regret, but now it was the time that was really worrying him.

He didn't need to dig out the member's card with which he had armed himself for the shop clerk, a man on the cusp of old age who had got to know him by sight over the years he'd been coming to the place, to pop out from the other side of the showcase beaming at him. The results of the test, he was informed, were that, while his sight had not declined as much as might be expected in someone whose first pair of reading glasses had been made here in his early fifties, some modification was needed. He also had a problem with astigmatism, so a new pair of lenses was recommended.

He was being treated so well that the agitation he'd felt since calling from the pay phone finally subsided and he ventured a little joke.

—Will they see me out?

—I am afraid that's unlikely, sir. We'll be looking forward to serving you again.

After this affable reply, the clerk tapped away on the small buttons of his calculator, told him what the new lenses cost, then waited in silence while he signed the credit card slip.

—That's a nice jacket you have on, sir.

He looked up to see the smiling clerk tugging at his own

123

lapels as he took the payment slip.

—You think so? I like it too. About my only good one.

—It suits you, sir. To a tee.

—Sure your glasses aren't playing tricks on you?

He looked at the other man, who was wearing stylish rimless glasses. He knew it was flattery, but it didn't hurt.

—There's no problem with my glasses, sir. I got them here.

—Since you've been kind enough to pay me a compliment, I feel I ought to keep an afternoon date.

Nonchalantly he slipped his hands into his side pockets. No piece of paper. His right hand encountered the handkerchief and the disposable lighter; the fingertips of his left one came into contact with the teeth of the small comb. The slip of paper, which he had folded in two after smoothing it out, was nowhere to be found.

—Looking for something, sir? asked the clerk sympathetically.

—No. Nothing important, he replied, shaking his head and trying to remember what he had done when he made the phone call. Had he held the thing in the same hand as the receiver while dialing the number, or did he put it on top of the phone? He wasn't sure, but the memory of what happened after she hung up had vanished completely. He had so little idea what he'd done with his hands after that feeling of being shoved out into the passageway, he might as well have left them behind too.

—I don't think you've dropped anything since coming in here, sir.

—The main thing was to pay you. The other one doesn't matter.

With a little bow to the still worried-looking clerk he left the shop. His legs made automatically for Tokyo Station. As he walked, he emptied his pockets and checked each item that emerged. His hands proceeded from his jacket to his

124

trousers, from his front to his back pockets, and finally dived into his chest pocket—but, sure enough, he couldn't find it. And yet, the telephone card he'd used to make the call was sitting quite demurely in his wallet.

As though a fine wire had suddenly snapped, regret thrummed inside him. The problem wasn't just his being able to call again—or not. The fact of having lost something was upsetting in itself; the worry it involved was physically painful, like being raked by a claw.

He checked his watch again when he reached the Yaesu entrance. He had used up thirty-five minutes on his visit to the optician's. His legs strode into Tokyo Station and, without giving him time to think what they were doing, proceeded along the passage that crossed the station to the Marunouchi exit on the opposite side where the new Maru Building stood. It wasn't because he had lost the piece of paper with the phone number that he was in such a hurry to get there. Even if he had the number in one of his pockets, he would definitely still have headed for the place the woman had designated. Losing the note was just the final spur to go there. It was obvious that if he met whoever it was on the terrace, the phone number wouldn't matter. He was more worried about failing to meet anyone and being left in the building without anything being properly resolved.

A huge construction rose in front of him when he emerged from the station canopy. With the afternoon sun serving as a backlight, it loomed over him, dominating his field of vision. He remembered the old Maru Building as a flattish, four-square building of eight stories, but what now confronted him was a towering structure that seemed to be shoving the sky above it out of the way.

What stopped it from looking too precarious was the broad and solid square base that went up to the fourth or fifth floor, from which a long cube extended further like a thick pillar. It looked as if someone had stuck one long building block on its end in the middle of a chunkier one. When he looked more carefully at the point where the two sets of blocks met—near the top of the base of the building, in other words—he could just make out a windowless, hollowed-out space. This, he assumed, was the terrace she mentioned. He felt as though he were on a beach staring at the tip of a promontory.

After waiting for the light to change, he crossed several lanes of traffic. His sole focus was on keeping his arms and legs moving toward the entrance of the vertical monolith. He was too preoccupied to think about what might happen once he reached the terrace.

The interior into which he stepped was not what he had expected. A bare open space with an unusually high ceiling and a hard, cold, unwelcoming atmosphere, it felt as if it were still under construction despite the large numbers of people there. Nobody seemed quite sure which way to go. Up ahead was an open area awash in sunlight—somewhere apparently for the air to play, an atrium that went up to the upper floors.

Noticing that an escalator to his right was sucking in a stagnant pool of people, he surrendered to the flow and stepped on as well. As he was propelled relentlessly upwards, a gleaming tableau of neatly displayed clothes, handbags, accessories, interior furnishings, and cosmetics appeared at eye level, then disappeared at foot level. The feeling that pervaded the place was strangely abstract and clear, with neither the bustling everyday ordinariness of a local department store nor the busy muddle of a neighborhood shopping street. It was so impersonal that it helped relieve some of the nervousness bearing down on him from the terrace above.

The instructions he'd been given about which floor had been rather vague, so he got off the escalator at four and made a circuit. His eyes were drawn to an elevator that went up and down inside a thick, transparent tube of plastic or reinforced glass in which the mechanical components could be seen. He was surprised to discover that the ground-floor atrium extended all the way to this floor, but despite traipsing around between the CD shops, the shoe stores, and the boutiques with lots of kids milling about, he could not find anything resembling a door onto a terrace.

He took a deep breath and stepped gingerly onto the up elevator. I don't know what's waiting for me up there, but I've obviously got to go. His mind was made up, but he also felt the calm of resignation. A sneering voice seemed to be pushing him from below. You're hardly going to be kidnapped and eaten, are you?

The atmosphere of the fifth floor, where all the restaurants were located, was completely different. The corridor heaved with middle-aged people whose expressions declared a frank intent to get some food in their bellies—an urge different from the shopping impulse—and the come-ons from the restaurant greeters washed around them in languages that sounded unfamiliar, strange. As he stepped, half-propelled, off the escalator, wondering skeptically why the place should be so crowded when it wasn't even lunchtime, he saw the sky on the other side of a tall pane of glass in front of him. The backs of people leaning on a green handrail and looking down formed an unbroken line on both sides.

That's the terrace, he thought, startled at how wide it was, before passing quickly through the automatic doors and out onto the wooden decking. The air was piercing. He had forgotten how cold it was. Wish I'd worn a coat, he thought for the first time. Might protect me from other things than the cold too.

Forcing himself to look away from all the people's backs, he confronted the vast and cloudless sky. A cowardly little impulse drifted through him: Might be better if I just paid my respects to the sky and headed home.

It was when he was standing with his arms crossed beneath a young tree that emerged from a round hole in the wooden decking, thinking that he would just have to wait for the woman to find him as there was no way for him to find her: an elderly couple—married, he guessed—broke from the row of backs, turned around, and slowly moved away from the railing toward him. He briefly tensed up, but the two of them walked past him with bored-looking, wizened faces. He felt himself drawn to the space, which was already starting to narrow, between two sets of shoulders, and slipped in.

As he leaned against the metal rail, at chest height with transparent plastic panels beneath, the long brick sun-illuminated mass of Tokyo Station spread out before him, with tiny little taxis trundling about between the flowerbeds dotted with yellows and reds in front of it. Beyond the dark roof of the station he could see the white upper stories of the Daimaru department store. Over on the left, where the long red and white arm of a crane floated, must be where the old National Rail Building had once stood. If he went up to the top thirty-somethingth floor here, he'd obviously get a fabulous view of Tokyo Bay.

Captivated by the view, he leaned out over the rail for a moment, his face directly exposed to the cold wind which was blowing in sharp, regular little gusts. Feeling some pressure on his right shoulder, he turned in surprise. A plump man in a Tyrolean hat with a white feather stuck into the ribbon was trying to take something out of the pocket of his short coat. The wind blew the sound of a soft laugh at him from the left side. A woman in a black coat with a long, glossy fur collar stood beside him.

—The old Maru Building had eight floors, so you should have been able to get the same view from there too.

128

The comment, somewhere between a murmur and a whisper, emanated from the fur of the wind-ruffled collar.

—But it didn't have a terrace.

Seduced by the softness of her voice, his answer came automatically. She was so close to him that he could only make out a vague profile, but from her hair, which was heavily streaked with gray, and her self-possession, he guessed she was about the same age as him.

—The bottom floor wasn't so blank and bare either.

—Do you remember that antique china shop on the corner?

He saw in his mind's eye the dull red of the saucers and teacups in the display window.

—The bookshop opposite . . . Fuzanbo, wasn't it?

His company's head office had been nearby. He was in charge of a factory, but when he had to attend important meetings he would often pass through the Maru Building on his way there and back, but the first-floor ceramics shop was about all he could remember. Still, it wasn't unpleasant to take his cue from the woman's nostalgic recollections. He couldn't tell if the person who stood beside him was the person he'd been speaking to on the phone. The low, slightly husky voice certainly sounded similar, but coming to any sort of conclusion was difficult. Was it normal for two people who had just bumped into one another to fall so naturally into conversation? Maybe it's better I don't know, he had just told himself, when the woman addressed him in an even quieter voice. Her shoulder had moved a little closer.

—Would you have come this far if it hadn't been a woman who answered the phone?

The question had come out of left field. He was at a loss. She seemed to disregard it as she leaned out toward the red and white arm of the crane and the half-built building. The black fur on her collar quivered in the wind.

—I probably wouldn't . . .

—Why not?

—That's just how I felt.

He couldn't really understand what had happened after he made the call. And what led up to his making it in the first place was even more of a mystery. Nonetheless, he found it impossible to believe his standing here next to her was any kind of mistake.

—Wonder if this was all underwater in ancient times.

The woman drew back a little and slowly swiveled her head from side to side a little as though contemplating an expanse of water. As he'd thought, the handsome, oval face he got a glimpse of belonged to someone he'd not met before.

—And in not quite so ancient times it was a moor covered in tall wild grass.

—Wonder if there were foxes and raccoons running around.

—Snakes and field mice.

—And it all ends up forgotten, right?

The woman spoke in a harsher tone, staring stiffly ahead.

—I'm not really too sure . . .

Feeling under attack, he equivocated nervously.

—So, shall we be going?

The words were spoken hurriedly not to him but to a second woman who was standing on her other side, dressed in a coat the color of autumn leaves. It had never occurred to him that she might have a companion, and he reacted with blank amazement. The first woman retreated from the rail and moved away. The other woman, the one in the long coat, soon caught up with her and turned back to look at him. She appeared to be about the same age, but he had never seen her before either. He thought she ducked her head very slightly at him. The movement was so subtle it wasn't clear whether she was saying good-bye on behalf of the person he'd been talking to, or warning him not to follow them. Passing between a couple of saplings poking up from the decking, the two of them went through the door and rapidly disappeared in the crowd of people. The cold assaulted him, suddenly and brutally. It seemed to tear all the natural warmth out of his body. His soft wool jacket could not protect him. The wind had picked up and was blowing directly onto the terrace. His line of sight was blocked by people scurrying back into the building. When he turned back to look over the railing again he saw the yellow ginkgo leaves that had been swept up from the little garden in front of the station dancing as they caught the sun.

To get home he took the escalator to basement level and hurried along the broad underground walkway to Tokyo Station. The desire to get away from the pair of women on the terrace was intense. He couldn't put his finger on any one thing, but the feeling was based on a combination of suspicion, speculation, bewilderment, and fear, that he could feel rolling through him like a great, slow wave and which he had no choice but to accept. As he walked, his whole body swayed from one side to the other. When he lowered himself onto a warm seat in the train, which started at this station, he began to sneeze and couldn't stop.

—I see they've finished the new Maru Building, murmured his wife after dinner with no particular interest as she flicked through the evening paper.

—Oh, that was a few months ago now.

—Long before the original building went up, they say the area was a grass plain full of foxes and raccoons, stretching as far as the eye could see.

—You say there were raccoons?

He peered over at the newspaper his wife was reading to see if there was an article about the new building, but none of the photographs seemed to feature it.

131

—Where there are foxes, you generally find raccoons too, right?

—Raccoons tend to live in places in between, not cultivated land or really wild, either.

—I wouldn't know . . .

She sounded bored.

He had another fit of sneezing. His wife looked up and was about to say something, but ended up going back to her paper in silence.

He suddenly turned to look at his jacket, which had not yet been put away and was hanging on the wall of the next room. He had a feeling that there was something inside the chest pocket.

FOR THE RECORD

A Happy New Year
Wishing you all the very best for the New Year

(Mass-produced rubber stamp. The black ink on the stamp had come out as a faint gray. The rest of the note was scribbled in black ballpoint pen.)

I've broken off any involvement I had in "the cause."
I have five grandchildren now. Woe is me!

The first day of the first year of the twenty-first century
Tokyo

(Addressed to O.O. from Q.W. A New Year's card for 2001 including a lottery number: group B2563 215856. Not a winning number.)

***

Dear All,

I hope you are well.

It's nearly time for the cherry blossom party of the Ten Man Strong Club. Some of you may be wondering what's going on, seeing as I haven't yet sent out any details about this year. That's why I'm getting in touch now to let you know how things stand.

I have actually had a bad back since around the end of January and am still not able to walk. I went to the hospital and had all sorts of tests, none of which helped pinpoint the cause of the problem. I also tried massage, acupuncture, moxibustion, and deep breathing exercises, all to no effect, and ended up being told it might clear up as the weather gets warmer.

If that was the only problem, all I'd need would be to get someone to take over my job as organizer for this year, but B, as part of his post-retirement consultancy, is scheduled to be in Canada from the end of March to the beginning of April. S is busy taking care of his wife, who isn't well, and N has arrhythmia and doesn't want to leave the house. In other words, we've got a whole host of problems on our plate. It would be sad if only four of the eight of us were able to get together, so I was thinking we might postpone our party and enjoy the autumn colors instead of the usual cherry blossoms.

As we only meet once a year it's an important occasion for all of us. I really hope we'll manage it this year too, but given the way things are I think we should just wait and see. What do you think?

We first started these get-togethers of ours in our mid-teens, and although there was a long gap in the middle, we've met once a year without fail for the last twenty years or so, making this a tradition I don't want us to break. It's actually been over half a century since we began. There's nothing much anyone can do about physical decline, but let's all try and do our best so we can be in good health to meet this autumn.

(Dated March 5. Printed on a sheet of A4. Up to this point the text from T.T. was printed horizontally using a word processor or PC. In the space underneath was a handwritten note to O.O. written in blue-black ink with a fountain pen.)

P.S. There's no need to worry about my back. I can grin and bear it. When I was a kid, I suffered from nasty growing pains in my legs, now the opposite is happening with my back. Apparently N's arrhythmia is nothing too serious either. I suspect he's depressed. His voice on the phone was rather listless. I assume you're okay, but be careful anyway since we've reached an age where one doesn't know what might be around the corner. C is toiling away growing daikon on the land he leased, G is having fun going to the movies with his senior citizen discount. Q.W. folded up his little democratically managed business that caused him so much trouble, and is probably casting around for something new to do now. That means we've lost the only company president the Ten Man Strong Club ever had.

***

I got a note from T.T. about postponing the annual get-together. I suppose you got it too? Everyone goes on about the new millennium, and here we all are going to pieces physically. It's a shame. In a P.S., he said you had quit being a boss and were looking for something new to do. I remember the New Year's card you sent. For you, I know that finding something to do isn't about the routine of everyday life. It's about making up for lost time and working for a fairer social system—what you once referred to as your mission in life. That's what you should try to keep doing. Whether it's feasible or not I really don't know . . . Anyway, I'm looking forward to hearing what you have to say in autumn when the Ten Man Strong Club (there are only eight of us left now) gets together. Don't overdo the boozing!

137

(Dated March 11. Addressed to Q.W. from O.O. Pre-stamped post office card, blue ink, handwritten in vertical lines.)

***

Tuesday, May 15. A bright day. Low 19°C High 24°C.

There's a dry wind blowing. Feels like early summer. I'm going about in a T-shirt.

Unable to resist the good weather, I went out with Asako, who was going to Nihonbashi to do some shopping. As I didn't want to go to the department store with her, we went our separate ways and I got off at Ochanomizu by myself. I had this sudden urge to make for the Hijiri-bashi Bridge to the east of the station. Perhaps because it usually has so few pedestrians, it struck me as a "proper" bridge, which I'd be able to get a good view from.

Despite the warm weather, there was a fellow still in some sort of whitish half-coat, back hunched and head thrust out, coming toward me from the Yushima side. We were about to pass one another in the middle of the bridge, when it turned out to be N of all people! I remembered that the note about putting off the Ten Man Strong Club get-together had said he had arrhythmia, so I asked him how he was. Said he was on his way back from the hospital. He wouldn't talk about his symptoms frankly, and I got no clear answer. When I suggested having a cup of tea, he was noncommittal. But he didn't seem to be in a hurry to get away either and we leaned on the stone parapet and chatted halfheartedly while looking down at the muddy water below. The conversation drifted on to the subject of all the club meetings we hadn't been able to hold. The new leaves on the trees on the embankment waved gently under the powerful sun. Don't know if it's something to do with the tides, but the water, dotted here and there with bits of trash, seemed to have stopped completely.

—In the old days the nightsoil boats must have gone up and down this river, N suddenly announced.

I could just about remember them myself. I thought I'd heard they used to go out to sea and just pitch it all overboard, but I wasn't sure they used this river, the Kanda, or not.

—In Q.W.'s New Year's card it said he's broken off his involvement in "the cause," N muttered, apropos of nothing and as if he were talking about something that had only happened the day before.

—And I bet the card continued, "I have five grandchildren. Woe is me!" I chimed in. The guy wrote exactly the same thing to all of us, I thought a little sourly.

—Was there ever really any cause worth bothering about?

—Well, there was for Q.W. if no one else. He started tossing Molotov cocktails around without even going to university.

I didn't understand why N had suddenly brought up the subject, but I wanted to let him know how I felt when I read Q.W.'s note. I remembered Q.W.—thin, short, and barely changed from when he was a teenager—always toiling away as if trying to roll a huge stone up a slope. So with his five grandchildren around his feet, the image changed from something a bit pitiful to a more homely one. And it occurred to me that, for him, his mission in life was over.

—How many grandchildren have you got? I asked N, who had gone all quiet.

—I don't need grandchildren.

—It's your children who produce them. Granddads like us have no say in the matter.

—I still don't want any.

N flapped his hand at about stomach level and abruptly

strode off, saying, —Well, see you. Conversations with N tended to end like that. I nodded back and headed on toward Yushima. I looked back when I got to the end of the bridge, but I couldn't see him anymore. Maybe he'd turned off into the station.

I had some tempura noodles by myself, then went home. Asako wasn't back yet.

(O.O.'s diary. Blue ink covering two and a half pages of an old-fashioned university notebook, written with a pen in horizontal lines.)

***

You okay? My back finally stopped hurting. I came up to the mountain cottage yesterday. I was careful not to overdo it, but I cleaned the whole place up, so I can take it easy now. It's hot in the middle of the day but the mornings and evenings are pleasantly cool. Give me a call if it looks like you might be able to make it out here. Plan to spend the rest of July and the whole of August here and go back in September. I'll discuss the dates for the Ten Man Strong Club meeting with you then.

(Dated July 14, Bastille Day. Picture postcard from T.T. to O.O. Written in vertical lines with a fat-nibbed pen in blue-black ink. Picture on the front was Toshio Arimoto's oil painting, *Wood with Falling Blossoms*.)

***

Summer greetings,

With the spring get-together being postponed, it's been a long time since I last saw you. I persuaded several friends

140

to lease a new field in Yamanashi this spring. What I really wanted to do was to start growing rice from seedlings, but it's not easy so it will have to wait for next year. We did manage to produce plenty of vegetables, though—tomatoes, cucumbers, and garden peas. I'll send you some as there's too much for me to eat. We don't use any dangerous chemicals, so they're a lot more wholesome than the stuff you buy at the supermarket. Give my regards to your wife.

(Dated August 3. Addressed to O.O. on C's pre-stamped post office card. Neat lines of vertical writing in a black ballpoint pen.)

***

Dear All,

How have you been?

I've not been in touch since telling you about the postponement of our spring get-together a while ago. I hope you're all well.

I'm writing because I got a postcard from Q.W. at the beginning of the month announcing that he had cancer of the esophagus. It's not clear when it started, but he first went into a public hospital around June for radiation treatment and chemotherapy. Since the cancer is already in the lymph nodes, an operation is difficult. As well as being unable to speak, he's suffering from side effects like nausea. The postcard was in his usual illegible scrawl, though, so he may not be stuck in bed. No one answers when you call his house, but I suppose that's because his family are all visiting him at the hospital. I have absolutely no idea what the prognosis is. All we can do is hope that the radiation therapy and drugs work. He's always been pretty robust so I think he'll pull through.

I spoke with O.O. on the phone and we agreed that in this

141

situation it would make sense to wait a little longer before having the meeting we were planning for autumn.

I'm going to see him as soon as I can. I'll let you all know if I have any news.

It's a pity this has happened on the verge of my sending a letter saying we should get together in October. Not having heard anything from the rest of the gang, I assume they're getting on with their lives as normal. Anyway, let's take good care of ourselves. When even a man like Q.W., who's never had an illness worthy of the name in his life is laid up, it puts us all on notice.

(Dated September 5. Printed on a sheet of A4. Up to this point the text from T.T. was printed horizontally using a word processor or PC. In the space below was a handwritten note to O.O. written in blue-black ink with a fat-nibbed pen.)

P.S. I sent this letter to the rest of the group. As I said on the phone, I was really upset to hear that he's inoperable. Anyway, I'll let you know how he is after I've been to the hospital.

***

How have things been? I was relieved to hear from T.T. on the phone that you're gradually getting your voice back. It really wouldn't do for someone like you who's always got something to protest about in the affairs of this world of ours to be silenced! So get better soon and start speaking out. Let me know if there's anything I can do to help. I'll come and see you soon. Don't go and do anything silly just because you're feeling a bit better.

(Dated September 10. Addressed to Q.W. on O.O.'s pre-stamped post office card. Blue ink. Written vertically with a pen.)

***

Greetings,

It's a chilly autumn, but I hope this finds you all well.

I was hospitalized in late June with esophagus cancer and discharged on September 30 after completing a course of treatment that lasted over three months. It being cancer, I can't say I'm cured, but I managed to outfox the grim reaper and am now convalescing at home.

I know you were all worried about me while I was there. A sincere thank-you for all your encouragement and support. I just wanted to take this opportunity to let you know that I'm back at home.

(Dated 2001. Up to this point, the letter from Q.W. was on two pages of B5 paper with the text printed vertically in Mincho font. It was accompanied by a personal note to O.O. on two sheets of manuscript paper in black ballpoint pen.)

To cut to the chase, I'm alive and back on the outside. I know the Ten Man Strong Club were concerned about me, so please give them all my best. From what they told me when I left the hospital, my chances of survival had been fifty-fifty. Not the greatest odds. The treatment has powerful and unpleasant side effects but I put up with it by pretending I was being tortured by American imperialists. In some ways it's difficult to say outright whether my surviving was really a good thing. Subjectively speaking, I may have had a lucky escape, but the health of this country—as seen in the prime minister's servility to America etc.—is just getting worse and worse. When I read the paper or watch TV, it's hard to find a subject that doesn't make me mad.

Objectively speaking, why should a useless old codger like me keep on living? I have absolutely no intention of fading away quietly doing the gardening or something, but I also seem to have lost the desire to be of use to other people in the future. So it's only natural for me to ask why I survived. I can't speak for other people, but personally I think my doubts about it will stick with me for quite a while.

Sorry. I meant to write a note to thank you for your kindness but ended up going off the rails a bit. Chalk it up to illness. (My voice is still not quite right, so I won't be calling for a while.)

***

If you've already sent me something then this postcard will be too late, but I'm writing it anyway. I'm very grateful for your kind support since I got out of the hospital. T.T. sent me a vast amount of food, and the refrigerator is packed with his stuff, as well as the co-op deliveries. I'm part of a generation that can't throw away food uneaten, so in future please send me your kind thoughts but no actual things. I haven't yet recovered physically, and am trying not to lift or move even the lightest objects. That's my situation. Of course, having all these friends means a lot to me.

(Dated October 7. Addressed to O.O. Pre-stamped post office card from Q.W. Black ballpoint pen. Vertical lines.)

***

I've got something to report. This time it's fairly good news.

Q.W., who as I told you was in the hospital recently, got

144

out on September 30. Some of you may have already heard, but it's still worth repeating. The two courses of treatment he had seem to have worked. He had a tissue examination before leaving, but no cancer cells were found. He wrote to say he felt he was "lucky to survive." When I visited him in the hospital he was looking emaciated, but after getting out his appetite has improved and he's planning to start using his bike soon. His vocal cords are gradually recovering, so I'm hoping that we'll soon be able to hear him talking and laughing away (but for now, phoning him is still inadvisable).

The upshot is that this is yet another notice of postponement. I hope you'll all take good care of yourselves over the winter, and next spring we can have a grand get-together after this two-year break, with Q.W., who should be restored to health by then.

(Dated October 18. Up to this point the text from T.T. was printed horizontally on a sheet of A4 using a word processor or PC. In the space underneath was a handwritten note to O.O. written in blue-black ink with a fat-nibbed pen.)

P.S. I certainly feel a degree of relief but I can't feel entirely positive. Mentally he's tough, so all we can do is wait for him to recover through sheer strength of will. Am I being an old woman to think he'll go too far and have a bicycle accident or something?

***

Wednesday, November 21. Clear day. Low 8°C High 17°C.

The weather forecasters keep talking about an Indian summer and it certainly is warm. The glow of yellowing leaves on the neighbors' magnolia is reflected in the north-facing window up on our second floor.

145

The sunshine was so tempting, I went out for an early afternoon walk. Asako wasn't in when I got back and I noticed that the answer phone was flashing. It was T.T. with the news that Q.W. had been readmitted to the hospital. I called back, but he was out. I left a message, asking him to let me know if he heard anything.

(O.O.'s diary. Written horizontally in blue ink in an old-fashioned university notebook.)

***

Tuesday, November 27. Clear day. Low 8°C High 13°C.

The forecast said it would be cold today, but there's no wind so it's not that bad.

I went to the hospital this afternoon to visit Q.W. He was sitting there alone in his pale blue pajamas on his bed in a six-person ward. When he saw me, he said hello, but his voice was weak and hoarse. I asked if it was really all right for him not to be lying down. Lying for hours on end isn't much fun, replied that hoarse voice. T.T. told me Q.W. had been readmitted because he was completely unable to take any food, but his face didn't look that thin. I thought it was better for him not to speak so I did all the talking.

Hunched forward, he suddenly muttered, "It's hopeless. There's no way things can be sorted out properly." I looked at him to see if he was talking about disposing of his estate, but from his expression he obviously wasn't. I guess he meant his mission. "Don't worry about it," was the best answer I could come up with.

"Young people now are doing okay, they're doing the best they can. But me—what did I . . .?" The sun was so bright that he broke off, screwing up his face and asking me to pull the curtains shut. He stretched his hand toward the bedside

146

table and pointed, so I poured some water from the pot into a glass. He took a mouthful then straightened his neck and swallowed some of it. It looked very painful.

The sun was setting as I walked back, in preference to taking the bus, but after I couldn't figure out which direction the station was in, I took a passing taxi.

(O.O.'s diary. Blue ink in an old-fashioned university notebook. Horizontal writing with a felt-tip pen.)

***

I already telephoned, but I wanted to send a map of the place where Q.W.'s wake and funeral will be held to anyone who's coming. It's about ten minutes' walk from the station and easy to find. The ceremony will be non-religious.
Wake   December 5, 6–7 p.m.
Funeral   December 6, 1–2 p.m.

(B4 fax paper. Large characters written with a felt-tip pen. Horizontal writing. Plus another page with what looked like a printed map.)

***

Thursday, December 6. Rain. Low 8°C High 11°C.

This entry is two days in one.

The fifth, yesterday, the day of the wake, was cold. "I will arrange for some of the music the deceased held dear to accompany the offering of flowers," said the middle-aged undertaker. I stopped myself from saying, What the heck's this "held dear" got to do with him? Still, when a crackly recording of the "Internationale" came on, a shiver did go up my spine. I found myself looking around the room but

147

everyone else was expressionless. The voices in the chorus sounded tinny and far off. The "Internationale" was played several times, then the "Red Flag" until the tape ran out in the middle. I wonder if that made Q.W. angry or made him laugh? Probably he was looking down on this distant little world and its affairs and didn't give a damn. Maybe the cold was the reason why only four members of the Ten Man Strong Club were there. B rushed in just as the offering of the flowers was ending. He said a meeting had run late.

Today it rained from the morning on. There was a line of black umbrellas outside the funeral hall. Children from kindergarten to primary school age were playing in the waiting room before the funeral started. I counted seven of them; two in addition to his grandchildren. The one who seemed to be the oldest of the bunch was a boy of about eight. A mischievous little character, he was the spitting image of Q.W. I wanted to grab hold of him and ask him about his granddad but he was so busy chasing after the others that I couldn't get him to see me. Q.W.'s wife, who had a cold and was exhausted from looking after him, didn't say much. The two sons were both much taller than their father, and made me realize that Q.W. was the smallest man in the family. Obviously, though, he had thrown what little weight he had around and played the patriarch in his own home.

From one corner of the room where there was a cluster of three or four men in early old age, I heard a loud voice say, "I can't believe it—just when he was talking about how we should resurrect the western cell."

I was surprised when the old lady who delivered the eulogy, leaning on a cane and looking up at the photograph of the dead man, revealed that in his twenties, Q.W. had been very committed to the running of a local daycare center they had set up and had played a big part in looking after the kids on its sports day. He had always been fit, but given how much he'd despised P.E. and sports days and things like that at high school, it was unexpected.

Like yesterday, the crackly chorus of the "Internationale" was played during the offering of flowers and wasn't exactly easy listening, while the "Red Flag" again went funny in the middle. Were these songs really necessary? I was bothered by it, but then a funeral march wouldn't have fitted the bill any better either. The family consulted T.T., who then called me to ask my opinion. Now I regretted my stupidity in insisting on having the "Internationale." Frankly, I don't think the song exists that would send Q.W. peacefully on his way. I asked him if he thought silence would have been better and imagined him nodding in agreement.

In the coffin before it was carried outside, Q.W. was lying there with a very proper expression I'd never seen on his face before. His eyes were shut.

Seven members of the Ten Man Strong Club turned up.

(O.O.'s diary. Blue ink in an old-fashioned university notebook, horizontal writing with fountain pen.)

***

Dear Sir,

Thank you for making time to attend the funeral of the late Q.W. and for paying your last respects to the deceased despite all the other demands on your time.

(Printed thank-you letter.)

149

A DAY IN THE LIFE

It was raining and there was a long line of people waiting for the bus. The semicircular roof of the bus stop was only the length of a single bus so the people who couldn't fit inside stood there clutching their umbrellas in silence. Many of the umbrellas were black.

The bulky paper bag he had in his left hand was heavier than he'd expected, and having to hold the umbrella in his other hand to keep it dry was a strain too. He was warmly dressed, so the train had felt hot and stuffy. Now, after standing outside a while, he could feel the sweat cooling on his skin. Anxious about catching a cold again, he started to mark time gently where he stood. Keeping at least part of his body moving would probably slow the fall in his body temperature, he reckoned.

He had worked up a sweat helping his wife with the gardening on a crisp autumn afternoon a couple of weeks ago. Too lazy to get changed afterwards, he had caught a cold, with a temperature, and had to stay in bed. Not a pleasant experience. Even more unpleasant and irritating was the way his wife had laid into him, going on about how sloppy it was not to change his sweaty clothes and the risk of catching senile pneumonia. Somewhere along the line she had become quite unsparingly critical. Was she right? Had he become a genuine slob? Was she more short-tempered than before? Was it a combination of both things? Neither of them were getting any younger, so there was nothing he could do about it anyway.

The bus still hadn't come. Buses for different destinations furnished with gaudy advertisements and extravagantly sweeping windshield wipers, and buses painted in blue and red, arrived from time to time, but the one he was waiting for was a complete no-show. The arm supporting the umbrella and the arm holding the bag gradually grew tired and the muscles began to stiffen. He turned around and saw that there was now a longer queue behind him than in front. Some of the umbrellas ran out of patience and made for the taxi stand. He wasn't going far, so it wouldn't cost much—plus he had things to carry. Why not take one? No, I've waited so long already . . . he thought stubbornly, and continued with his little stepping motion.

From the outset, his plan for today had been something of a stretch. Even if the bus had come on time and he'd been able to complete one mission and get rid of his baggage, a second one, which obliged him to go back the other way to the city center by evening, remained. The two tasks had only fallen on the same day because he had kept procrastinating until he now found himself compelled to do both at the same time. Then it was raining. And the bus didn't come. Everything was turning out badly.

I'll need to make some adjustments to my plan to avoid things going haywire. He had brought his feet together and started doing some little jumps when a bus—he immediately recognized it as his because of the shortness of the name on the destination display—slowly pulled in from beside the bank. A little buzz of excitement passed through the line and there was a general pressing forward although the bus was still some way off. With its windows all steamed up, it eventually drew up and opened its doors. When the line began shuffling forward, he transferred his bag to the hand with the umbrella and used his free hand to search hastily in his jacket pocket for the hundred-yen and the ten-yen coins he would need. One less thing to worry about.

The road where he got off ran between fields and was hazy in the rain. He started walking. He guessed that the things growing in rows on the black earth were daikon and cabbages. The clumps of trees in the park beyond were blurs of gray. No reds or yellows, so perhaps they were mostly evergreens. When he finally got inside the building's deep portico, his trouser cuffs were sodden and rigid with cold.

Turning his back on all the bored-looking people seated in the lobby, he hurriedly wrote his name in the visitors' book at the reception desk, went around a nearby corner, and proceeded down a long corridor. He passed a number of doors with wheelchairs outside, then knocked lightly on one after checking the nameplate. Since she never heard him knocking anyway, he just grabbed the knob and went in.

—Happy birthday.

A small back was sitting in a chair facing a small television which was off. The back, bathed in a dull gray light from the window, was completely motionless. A little red-haired doll was suspended about halfway down a cord that dangled from the fluorescent ceiling light and was loosely tied to the bed frame. He took hold of the girl's soft tummy and gave a gentle tug.

—Ah, here you are.

A croaky voice emerged from the face that slowly turned toward him.

—Happy birthday, he repeated in a louder voice while scanning the TV stand and the area around it for any sign of her hearing aid. She knew he was talking to her but couldn't make out what he was saying, so she pointed to the lower shelf in the stand. The hearing aid, which he dug out of a cloth bag with a drawstring neck, pee-peeped in his hand without him doing anything. It had been left on. She finally became

155

more herself after sticking the earphone in. He responded to her immediate complaint about the sound being on too high by turning down the dial.

—I wanted to give you that birthday present we discussed last time . . . I'm afraid I came alone—she's not well, her back started playing up yesterday.

—Well, I'm ninety-three now.

—Ninety-three? I thought it was ninety-five.

—No, I checked, see.

His mother wobbled as she rose to her feet so he took hold of her elbow to support her. He thought he could feel the bone inside. He picked up the cane to which she pointed and handed it to her. She walked with surprisingly steady steps over to a small chest and opened the top drawer. A large magnifying glass sat on a red and black family calendar. She flicked it open to the Quick Age Check chart on the inside cover and thrust it under his nose. Divided up by horoscopes, the chart was like nothing he'd seen before and he had trouble figuring it out. The only thing he really followed was the bold characters indicating people's ages expressed in completed years in the Western style in the boxes of the grid.

She reeled off the old Chinese names of the stars—Eighth White Soil Star and First White Water Star—and threw in an explanation of the sexagenary cycle for good measure. He couldn't quite understand how it all hung together. Still, if you traced the row of little numbers from the year of her birth in the early 1900s, you could see that, sure enough, this year's birthday made her ninety-five.

—How odd. I wonder why I got it wrong? she said.

—No need to worry. You're over ninety and still going strong, so it's good news either way.

She was alert for her age, nor had she ever gone through a phase of talking or behaving strangely, so he decided this

156

was a simple mistake and not worth dwelling on. He hadn't known she had this calendar and he had no recollection of her mentioning her birth star before. Maybe it was something one of her other visitors got her interested in.

—I hope this is all right. I really looked hard but I couldn't find anything I was sure you'd like.

She replaced the calendar with its detailed horoscopes in the drawer, put the magnifying glass on top of it, and shut the drawer, as though shutting her age away.

A feeble murmur floated from her mouth like smoke as he reached for the parcel on the bed.

—Am I really ninety-five?

—Can I open it for you?

He undid the pink ribbon, tore off the wrapping paper, and pulled out the contents. It was a violet gown packed in tissue paper, which he gently placed on her little knees as she sat in her chair.

It took a while for her to react. Her voice sounded as though she had just woken up.

—Take the tissue paper off.

The dainty object, which he unfolded and spread across his forearms, looked like a bouquet of flowers as it hung in a gentle arc beneath the ceiling light.

—If it's too long you might trip on the hem. We need to check.

—It's lovely.

—How about getting up and trying it on?

—No thanks. I'll do it later by myself. It looks nice and comfy, though.

His mother plucked softly at the quilted hem, then, with a less imperious gesture than before, indicated he should put it on the bed. Spread over the duvet, the gown gave a quiet radiance to the place. The sound of rain could just be heard in the overheated room.

157

—How about a nice cup of tea? she said.

His mother was about to get up but he eased her back into her chair by the shoulder.

—I can't stay long today. I have to go off to Ginza.

—Ginza?

—Do you remember Kubodera? He used to come round to our house in Mejiro all the time?

—The one who became a university professor?

—That's right. His son has a photo exhibition on and today's the last day.

—The one who turned up with a kitten in his pocket?

—Yes, when we were both at university. Anyway, he's in the hospital at the moment, and he rang to ask me to go to his son's exhibition.

—I'm ninety-five? Really?

Wholly irrelevant to their present conversation, the question emerged in a voice that seemed to come from somewhere deep inside her. He got to his feet, pretending not to have heard.

—I'll come and stay longer next time. Is there anything you want me to bring?

He suddenly noticed she had removed her hearing aid and had wound the thin cord round and round her finger. When did she do that? Just as he was trying to get her to put it back in her ear so he could say a proper good-bye, someone knocked on the door.

—Mrs. Akimoto. Some flowers have come for you.

Along with the singsong voice, he glimpsed a burst of red, white, and yellow through the partially open door. Behind it was a young woman's face.

—Oh, I didn't know you had a visitor.

She wore an apron and seemed a bit flustered as he relieved her of the flowers. There was a large picture of a kangaroo on the front of the apron.

158

—Thank you. Today's her birthday, you see.

—Good heavens. Many happy returns. I had no idea. And how old are we?

—She's ninety . . . three.

Well, she's in great shape. Much healthier than plenty of younger people.

He immediately kicked himself for not giving her true age, but the woman, perhaps feeling bad about barging in on a family visit, gave a polite bob of her head and quickly left the room. He didn't recognize the name on the card that had come with the flowers. When he informed his mother of the name and handed her the bouquet, she ducked her head without getting up and thanked him as if he were the giver.

—How lovely. Isn't everybody kind, he sang out as if he'd picked up the chirpy way of talking of the young staffer who had delivered the flowers.

—Ninety . . . five, his mother whispered, mimicking the reply he had given about her age a little earlier.

But she couldn't have heard me, he thought.

He wrote his time of departure in the visitors' book and with a silent bow to someone he could see over in the office he left the building, as though making his escape. He would normally have had to listen to his mother's endless droning reminiscences about the old days without knowing exactly when they happened or who the remote characters featured in them really were, no matter how often these relatives or whatever were mentioned. Today he had unilaterally excised that part by leaving a lot earlier than usual. He nonetheless felt distinctly tired when he opened his umbrella and set off. Neither the rain nor the present he had lugged along were to blame; it must have been the brevity of his visit and the guilt of having stolen two years of life from his mother, and this weighed down his legs as he walked between the fields.

A clump of tubular white flowers he hadn't noticed on his

159

way there drooped at the roadside by the edge of a plowed field. He remembered having heard the name "angel's trumpet" somewhere. Presumably it came from the way the flowers widened out at one end. It looked as though there were several of the rain-battered trumpets on a stalk, but they stayed stubbornly quiet and no sound came his way. He also remembered having seen a photo of a similar plant in the paper where it was called "Korean morning glory." Maybe they were two names for the same thing, he wasn't sure. The newspaper article had said it was poisonous. He stopped by the wet flowers, which came up to his chest, and lit a cigarette, something he'd been restraining himself from doing ever since leaving home. Even the smoke felt damp and stuck in his throat.

The bus for the station appeared at the end of the road. It was earlier than he'd expected. Throwing his cigarette, which was down to the filter, into the empty can that served as the bus stop ashtray, he clambered on board and lowered himself into a seat, grateful for the chance to take it easy at last. To purge his head of the visit to his mother, he gave it a shake, and got ready for Ginza. He remembered how his parents used to take him to the Fujiya at Ginza 4-chome for lunch when he was a boy. He couldn't help imagining that what awaited him in the rain beyond was not the modern Ginza with all the big brand name stores but the traditional place, looking just as it did in the old days.

However, when he began making his way along the wet sidewalk with the invitation his friend's son had sent him in his hand, nothing was as he had thought it would be. There were fewer people than he had expected in the rainy, late-afternoon streets, and when he turned left at the Ginza 4-chome crossing, where the Wako and Mitsukoshi department stores are, onto the street that goes to Kyobashi, there were noticeably fewer umbrellas about. Once he got past

160

Matsuya department store, he was unfamiliar with the buildings, which wouldn't have been the case going the opposite way toward Shimbashi. He stopped so that he could get his bearings on the little map on the invitation card, and pivoted this way and that as he tried to work out where he was. His destination appeared to be squeezed somewhere between Ginza Avenue (which changed its name to Chuo Avenue halfway along) and Showa Avenue off to the east.

Deciphering the tiny letters on the map was not easy, but he committed the name of the building containing the gallery to memory, made a rough guess, and headed off down a side street. He was surprised at how quiet the area suddenly became. He encountered the odd cafeteria-style restaurant or old-fashioned coffee shop, but almost no flashy shops, just endless grubby buildings with sullen façades that gave little clue as to what was going on behind them.

There were even fewer pedestrians when he turned a second corner. It felt more like wandering the back streets of the East End than being in Ginza. In a kind of garage, a cargo of cardboard boxes that had been pulled out from beneath the tarp of a parked truck was being lowered to the ground. He went over and asked, but only got a "Hmmm" and a cocked head for an answer when he mentioned the name of the building.

Next thing he knew, he had come full circle and was back in the same place. The truck had gone, but he remembered the green logo on the sides of the boxes in the pile. It suddenly seemed absurd to be going to so much trouble hunting for the place in the rain. An old friend on his sickbed asking him to go had been hard to refuse, but he had only met the son two or three times. Once, he'd been asked to help him find a job and had set up a meeting with a friend, but in the end nothing came of it. Just because the same young man—now a lot less young, after going from one short-term job to

161

another without getting steady employment—was holding a photo exhibition, why should he of all people have to humor the doting dad? His wife had said exactly the same thing when he told her he would be trekking to Ginza after seeing his mother, and having to acknowledge she was right only made him all the more annoyed.

He stood there feeling as though he'd been made a fool of. Even the rain here in Ginza seemed worse than the rain before, falling on the trumpet flowers. I should just have a cup of tea, recharge my batteries, and head off home, he told himself. But then all the time and effort he'd spent so far would be wasted. It was so frustrating. He was about to scrunch up the postcard in his hand when it occurred to him that the phone number of the venue was probably on it. Following the map had been difficult, but if he got through on the phone he could use the line like Ariadne's thread to find his way. Even if finding a pay phone around here looked unlikely, he was sure to bump into one if he retraced his steps to Chuo Avenue. Before he could put this plan into action, however, he noticed a ray of light coming from a lone building at the end of the darkening alley. He was certain he'd gone that way just now, but perhaps the light hadn't been on then. The reddish tinge to it made him think of a lantern in the porch of a farmhouse beckoning lost travelers at night.

He was drawn toward it. Soon, in front of him, was a large plate glass window facing the street; in one corner of the interior, which looked almost darker than the street outside, hung a bare daylight bulb. Looks like a charcoal dealer's, he thought. Must be because everything inside was a grimy black.

Screwing up his eyes, he could make out several cubes of different sizes arranged on the floor and some imposing branch-like objects jutting from the walls. Feeling there was something contrived about the scene, he realized that

162

the whole space was a species of display. The silhouette of a smallish woman passed in front of the dark wall. Yes, it was an art exhibition and the building was a gallery!

Going past the window to try and find the entrance, he found an old-looking cast metal plaque sunk into the wall by the door, one side of which was open. On it was the name he had memorized from the postcard. He heaved a sigh of relief and vigorously shook the raindrops off his folded umbrella onto the floor.

Lit by a fluorescent light in the ceiling, the entranceway was empty and showed little sign of use. There was a rack of relatively new mailboxes along one wall and the door of an elevator opposite. A dim memory that it had been the fourth or fifth floor prompted him to press the up button. He took the invitation out of his pocket to confirm it was the fifth, but still the doors did not open. The needle on the semicircular display was stopped pointing at the first floor, but the doors didn't budge. In the semidarkness he eventually spotted a handwritten message on a piece of paper stuck on the wall by the button. *Anyone for the upstairs floors (2-5), please take the stairs at the back.* It seemed funny that the elevator had refused his bid to get to the fifth floor even though it had no idea where he was heading.

Reluctantly he went around to the stairs. With its high steps it was a difficult climb and his legs felt worn out by the time he got past the second floor. There was a single wooden chair of the kind used at primary schools on the third-floor landing. When he got to the fourth floor, he couldn't help collapsing onto a similar chair there. All he could hear was the sound of himself panting. If I keeled over here, it'd be half a day before anyone found me. His reluctance to believe that there was a place open to the general public somewhere above him intensified.

His knees were trembling by the time he made it to the

163

fifth floor. After leaning on the wall for a while to catch his breath, he gingerly made his way down a narrow corridor. There were a number of doors on one side. Next to one of them stood a table with some pamphlets on it and some low plants arranged on the floor with a bright light behind them. It was so quiet he suddenly felt afraid of being trapped in there.

He held his breath and opened the door. A girl promptly slid out through the narrow gap. Avoiding him with a twist of her torso, she skipped off down the passage. Coming across another human being after so long a time canceled out any offense he might have taken. He peered into the room with the clatter of someone running down the stairs at his back. In front of a single row of colorful photographs on the wall stood a tall man in a black sweater with his arms crossed. Their eyes met, but the other person gave no clear sign of recognition, instead retreating a couple of paces into the corner. He could only remember that Kubodera's son was tall, not what he looked like. He relaxed a little at the thought that having come this far all he needed to do have a quiet look around and then go home.

As far as he could tell, all the photographs were out of focus. Human bodies dissolving and flowing off to one side at funny angles; trees all listing in the same direction; even buildings that were blurred and out of shape. Kubodera had told him that the exhibition was the result of a long stint in Europe, so he had automatically assumed there would be towns, churches, and landscapes. He felt a bit confused to find his expectations so off the mark.

—Er-hem, came a muffled voice from somewhere behind his head. He turned to face the other man who timidly said his name.

—That's right, your father called me from the hospital.

—It's kind of you to come.

164

Something in the swarthy face with its thrust-out chin revived a distant memory of the slightly dopey university student.

—I notice everything's in flux.

—I took them all with a digital camera with a one-second exposure.

—Why one second?

—I was curious about how much people move in that time.

—You've got some buildings and trees in them too.

—But people are my main subject. Sometimes I deliberately move the camera. Because our eyes move.

—A second. Is that a long or short time?

—For a photograph it's a long time, but from a human perspective, well . . .

—Hardly one or two years.

—It's something I want to explore more.

Once they got chatting, the man proved surprisingly intelligent. It was more than ten years ago that there had been problems about him finding a job. The thought of that distant time made him smile wryly.

There was real passion in his voice as he talked him through his pictures one at a time. A woman walking in front of a huge poster, the artwork and the person fused together strangely so that you couldn't tell where the poster ended and the person began. A scene of a restaurant where lush colors harmonized like a piece of music, while the outline of a single face hovered like a refrain off to one side. It struck him that the essence of the work lay in the subtle disparity between things that were moving and things that weren't, and he ventured to express his interpretation.

—Yes. Here, take a look at this.

The fellow pointed to a photograph which showed a commanding view of a square somewhere taken from a

165

second- or third-floor window. It was either a cloudy afternoon or almost evening and a number of people, half dissolved into currents of air, flowed amidst the drab colors.

—The legs are in focus.

He only became aware of it now that it had been pointed out. There was a throng of normal, human legs with no bodies attached to them walking on the flagstones.

—I see what you mean. The legs stay behind.

He felt like slapping his knees.

—After you take a step and your body is going forward, there's a moment when your back foot is still on the ground.

This tall figure solemnly performed an exaggerated, slow-motion walk. Sure enough, the shoes always lagged a bit behind.

—Where are you in that interval?

—Where are you . . . ? the man said, thoughtfully cocking his head. The slightly unnerving idea that some part of you was left behind took hold of him. A physical sense of unwholeness, as though part of his body were sick. To walk with one foot always left to catch up . . . He'd been walking that way ever since leaving home that morning . . .

There was a rustling sound and the gray curtain by the door was pushed to one side. He was flustered by the sudden appearance of someone else in a room where before it had been just the two of them. A woman in early old age wearing a black dress that went down to her ankles stood there holding a tea tray. Acknowledging him with her eyes, she looked around before putting the tray on a round wooden stool.

—This is the gallery's . . .

Sounding a little jittery, Kubodera's son introduced the woman, who was the owner, but he couldn't catch her name.

—I'm afraid I can't offer you a seat.

166

—I'll have my tea like this. It's fine.

He stopped her picking up the tray she'd just put down on the stool and took one of the delicate teacups.

—This is such a small place.

—It's just the right size. Quiet. I like it.

He stood opposite her beside Kubodera's son, who had retreated a little. She had fine features, and the healthy glow of her complexion suggested she was younger than him. Why then did she give the impression of being his senior?

—Originally it was an apartment.

—An apartment . . . ?

—This building is an apartment block from the mid-1920s.

—Here in Ginza?

She told him the exact date. He was startled to hear it had been built in the year he was born. He didn't want to reveal that he and the decrepit building were the same age.

—There are still two or three families living here. They tend to be a little on the old side, of course.

—And some of the vacant flats are being used as galleries?

—There are other similar places around here.

—Old apartment blocks?

—There's the Dojunkai in Harajuku. That's the same sort of idea.

—Living somewhere like this would certainly be convenient. The stairs are a bit of an ordeal, though.

—Didn't you use the elevator?

Kubodera's son, who had been on the sidelines of the conversation, joined in.

—The notice said to take the stairs to the fifth floor.

—Oh no, it's fine, you can take the elevator.

He glanced at her to see what kind of expression was on her face.

167

—But the doors don't open. I tried to take it up here, but they refused to open.

—With those old elevators, you open them by hand.

Stifling a laugh, the woman mimed prizing something apart. He was embarrassed that the thought had never occurred to him.

—Ha! You have to pull them open.

—That's the way we do things. Here, at least.

The woman smiled sympathetically. He looked away from her and pretended to be examining the photographs on the walls again.

—He's an old friend of my father's, the son blurted out as if he had only just remembered the fact.

She nodded, a smile still on her face.

—Thank you. I enjoyed myself, he said by way of farewell as he made for the door. The two of them ducked their heads at him. He hadn't been there long, but he felt a strong urge to stay. Maybe to leave the place he'd have to shoot out like the girl he'd met on the way in. Too shy to stand waiting for the elevator in front of them, he put his hand on the railing and went slowly down the stairs, a step at a time. The thought came to him: if I walk like this, maybe my body and legs will stay together.

It was already dark in the rainy back street. The fatigue that had been building since he left home that morning suddenly hit him. Ninety . . . five: his mother's murmuring voice sounded quite lifelike inside his head. Where had she put those two years she had forgotten about? The image of the square where only the legs remained drifted up through the rain. His legs felt heavier when he turned the corner and he saw the headlights of the cars running along the main road. He wondered vaguely what age his mother would claim to be when next year's birthday came around. The wife and home he was going back to; the facility his mother lived in on the

168

road that ran through the fields; the room with the photos he had just left—they all felt far off, somewhere beyond the rain. Only the legs remain. Only the legs remain, he muttered to himself as his body stumbled on.

A ROUGH OLD DAY

From first thing that morning nothing went quite right.

While he was shaving for the first time in four days, he botched the stroke from his left cheek to his upper lip. He had just inserted a new blade into his razor and he felt a sharp pain in the wing of his nose. It was a pure, penetrating sensation. He didn't have his glasses on, so he couldn't be sure what had happened, but when he pressed his fingertips to the area that hurt they soon turned red, and a slightly lighter-colored liquid was dripping down into the basin on the washstand. When he removed the tissue paper he'd frantically applied to soak up the blood, he saw a round, irregular cut on his nose. Sometimes he nicked himself near his lips and on his chin, but he couldn't remember ever having done it to his nose. As he applied tissue after tissue, the flow of blood stopped, but the cut, which ran from the fleshy swell of the side of his nose down to the bottom of his flat, squashy nostril, was like the mark of a crimson seal. Since his face was round and he had little in the way of hair, the figure confronting him in the mirror looked like a silly old man ready to squat down and launch into a silly rustic dance.

He had gouged off only the outermost layer of skin together with a little of the flesh, the cut not being deep, but he still told himself off for not being more careful on what was an important day for him. He remembered what his grandmother, who had lived with them when he was a boy, had told him. Grandma, who had been born in the 1880s, worried seriously about things that happened in the morning. If something bad happened early in the day, it was a case not only of "What happens twice, happens thrice," but—decisively—the "Third time is always the worst," meaning the prospect of some irreversible piece of bad luck. If crows cawed in the morning, she wouldn't leave the house. If one of the thongs on her clogs snapped on her way out of the place, even on a fine day she would turn pale, go back indoors, and kneel before the household altar which held Grandpa's mortuary tablet and burn some incense there.

Even as a child he hadn't believed everything his grandmother told him, and the older he got the more he tended to dismiss it as mere superstition; but once he passed the age Grandma had been when she died, he noticed that her comments on all sorts of things would pop into his head out of the blue. Whether or not he believed what she said, he was physiologically attuned to her voice.

Usually he could get away without shaving more than once in the course of a normal, not-too-bothersome week, but today was different. And he had every reason to be nervous. He was scheduled to go to a hospital in the city center to have a second internal checkup, since he hadn't been feeling quite right inside for a while now. The doctor had told him to go for a CT scan first, then come in to see him.

There being no rubbish collection that morning, no crows were squawking, but the razor episode was probably a more dire omen than they could ever be. He thought about using some adhesive plaster with gauze to conceal the wound, but couldn't figure out how to stick it on the abraded skin along the side of his nose. With the small consolation of knowing that at least the bleeding had stopped, he strolled into the living room and lit the first cigarette of the day.

—Quite sure you're allowed to smoke before your checkup? his wife said disapprovingly from the kitchen.

—If it's okay for me to eat, why shouldn't I be allowed to smoke? he replied, then spread the paper open on the breakfast table. Tens of thousands of chickens had been slaughtered at one go in an effort to stop the spread of bird flu. He wondered if the chickens had had any forewarning as they pecked away at their final meal. An omen affecting tens of thousands of lives would have to be something major . . .

—What's wrong with your nose? asked his wife suspiciously. She had brought in a bowl of rice and some plates and gestured for him to take the paper off the table.

—I gave myself a bit of a nick.

—But you've got no stubble there.

—Do I look odd?

—It's a look that not even a clown would go for.

—Should I put on a surgical mask to go out?

—No, it would chafe and make the cut hurt.

She only needed to say the words for his nose to start hurting. Instinctively he gently covered it with one cupped hand. The ash broke off the end of the cigarette he had in his other hand and fell onto his trousers. Just his luck. A red point glowed in the middle of the little heap of ashes. Before his wife could notice, he hastily returned the cigarette to his lips and swept the ash into his hand. It hadn't felt hot, but a dark spot had appeared on the gray polyester-mix cloth; when he worried it, a small hole opened up in his trouser thigh. He caught his breath: was this the day's second bit of bad luck already? His granny was particularly nervous about the third slipup. When he was a boy, she had told him that bad things always came at you thick and fast, but that you can get to three and have done with it by pretending to trip up. Now that he had been living for a good while himself, he'd come up with a theory from his own experience: one unpleasant experience always led to four or five more in the same day. He wasn't afraid of the next specific mishap but

175

the whole wave of nasty incidents, big and small, that would pummel him throughout today. And an unusually large wave was building and threatening to break over him: when the forbidding doctor in his white coat spun around in his swivel chair.

—If it's anything important, I'll call and tell you, he said to his wife on his way out.

—Don't bother. You made such a fuss about nothing last time, she said by way of encouragement out in the hall. She was referring to a similar incident a few years ago. He didn't reply, "But I'd not cut my nose or anything like that then." Nor did he say, "I hadn't burned a hole in my trousers with my cigarette." Averting his eyes from the oval mirror on the wall, he hurriedly pulled open the front door.

As he went down the road to the station, he took care to walk inside the painted white line demarcating the sidewalk. He turned around frequently, alert not only to the risks posed by cars and trucks coming up from behind, but ready to react to the silent approach of bicycles. When he noticed a young man on a bike bowling toward him, talking loudly into the cell phone in his hand, he stopped and pressed himself against the hedge at the side of the street, waiting for him to pass.

He was about to get going again when a broken branch in the thick holly hedge that bulged out onto the street brushed his face. It didn't go into his eye, but the hard end of a branch snagged the arm of his glasses. They rode up on his forehead, but luckily didn't come off. Had they fallen onto the asphalt, the plastic lenses might not have cracked but they'd certainly have been scratched.

Thank God it didn't go into my face, he thought. Adjusting his glasses, he assured himself that what had just happened was one lucky event in a series of unlucky ones and definitely not a mishap. If the tip of the branch had stabbed him in the forehead or scraped the side of his nose which he'd just cut, blood might have been drawn for a second time. Looked at like that, it suggested his luck could be starting to change for the better. Hope rose inside him like a watery sun.

When he got to the station, he stayed away from the steep stairs that led up to the ticket gates (he had once tripped on the top one), and instead went around to the side to wait for the elevator. There was a young mother also waiting in front of the closed doors. She was holding a baby, which he guessed she had just lifted up out of its pushchair. The small, soft-looking face, buried deep inside a hood, was turned toward him; the hands were twitching inside the sleeves; the extraordinarily large pupils of the pure black eyes stared at him unblinkingly. A burbling came from the slobber-wet mouth.

—How's it going? he muttered to it with a jerk of his chin. The baby wasn't especially lovable but he felt he had to do something in return for being stared at for so long. He even gave a gentle shove to the handle of the pushchair when the elevator doors slid open.

The wan-looking mother nodded her thanks, then, noticing how fixedly the baby continued to stare at him, rocked it comfortingly from side to side. "Look at the nice old man. What a nice old man," she murmured in a singsong voice, giving him a quick smile.

His being an old man was not in dispute, but being called it repeatedly was not wholly welcome. When it occurred to him that perhaps the cut on his nose was the reason he'd been stared at so enthusiastically, he forgot about the baby. If a nose too goofy-looking even for a clown was what had so riveted the baby, then he must be a walking freak show. The elevator stopped, the doors opened, and he sped off to the ticket gate without looking back. Ignoring the platform elevator, he grasped the handrail and went down the stairs as

177

if he were being pursued.

When he finally got on the train, which arrived late, he surveyed the interior as its stuffy atmosphere, quite different from outside, enveloped him. While he hunted for an empty seat, he was thinking that he needed to get physically used to the smell in here as fast as possible. If he couldn't adapt and had to put up with feeling uncomfortable for the more than forty minutes it would take to get into town, the train would be even more unpleasant a place than it already was, given how anxious he felt about his destination.

It was a train heading for the city center outside the rush hour, so there weren't that many people standing, nor did there seem to be any oddballs among the passengers lined up on the benches, and no one was talking too loudly. After completing a quick survey, his next move was to start slowly making his way toward what looked like a possible seat at the front.

He came to a halt by the special seats for the elderly and handicapped. The three-seater bench on one side was occupied by an elderly couple and a middle-aged woman with a paper carrier bag on the floor at her feet. On the opposite side was a space about half a person wide between a man in a blue suit, fast asleep and slumped forward over the black briefcase on his knees, and another with short hair in an egg-yolk yellow jacket the hem of which was spread out like fanned feathers around him. The gray fabric of the special seats, a different color to the normal ones, looked very tempting.

On a sticker on the window behind, under the phrase, "Please give up these seats to passengers who need them," was a row of silhouettes in bright green: a mother with a child on her knees, a woman with a swollen belly, a man with a cane bent double, and another with a crutch at his side. The thought flashed through him that he didn't rightfully belong to any of the four categories, since he wasn't actually

178

sick, just going to check the possibility that he might be. Still, though he could be lucky and get the all-clear, the bent figure with the cane was probably the best match in terms of age.

Had he spotted such a small space on a long seven-seater bench, he would probably not have tried to squeeze himself in. Creating the necessary space was a tortuous process that involved several people sliding along one after another. But the three-seater bench in front of him was different. The man in the suit at one end was asleep with his body pressed into the corner, so it was clear that if the big guy with his jacket unzipped would just pull the hem in off the seat and sit a little differently, he would have no trouble installing himself neatly between them.

The long legs in their light brown cotton pants were wide apart and stretched far into the aisle from beneath the yellow, soft-looking jacket. The man wore glasses with thick black frames, but busy as he was pressing buttons on a cell phone he held just above the navel of his orange T-shirt, he showed no sign of looking up.

Normally he wouldn't have been brave enough to say anything and would have moved discreetly into the next car. You never knew how someone was going to take being asked to move up, but standing hungrily before the lure of a half-space was just too undignified.

But this time it didn't turn out like that. A voice in the back of his head said, "Sit down," and propelled him forward. A thought came to him like a sudden article of faith: if I manage to sit down here without any major problems, my tests at the hospital will be okay too. He didn't make the opposite prediction based on things not going his way. It was a one-way prophecy.

He wasn't sure quite when it had become habitual, but the practice of linking his actions to trite predictions had

179

him completely in thrall. To take the left-hand ticket gate, for example, was asking for trouble; just in time, he would veer off course, bumping randomly into people as he made to exit through the right-hand barrier instead. When the phone rang, the idea that it would be bad news if he didn't manage to pick it up by the fifth ring would galvanize him, sending him charging down from the second floor. If he told himself, you don't want to meet anyone coming the other way before you reach that corner, he would break into a trot; and when he hung the washing out to dry at his wife's request, if he took it into his head that something awful would happen if he dropped a single clothespin in the course of carrying out the task, he would do the job very slowly, handling each peg with excessive care. He knew perfectly well how trivial the situations were, and since he never analyzed what happened when he failed to fulfill his self-imposed conditions, the whole thing was meaningless. All the same, when a bee flew into his bonnet, it was impossible for him to ignore or evade it. He would sometimes ruefully reflect that this particular method of telling his fortune was not something to which even his over-superstitious grandma had introduced him, and he was afraid that his starting to behave regularly in so ridiculous a way corresponded with a waning of his life-force. Nonetheless, he remained firmly in thrall to this nonsensical practice and was incapable of casting off its yoke.

Right now the impetus of the wager he had made with himself had seized control and developed its own momentum. Most unusually, he could picture the result of the bet—as a shadow in his CT scan.

—Excuse me. I'd like to sit here, he said in a crisp tone of voice, leaning down toward the man in the jacket. Perhaps he didn't hear? The other fellow didn't move a muscle. His eyes remained fixed on his cell phone.

—Could you move up and let me sit down?

He tried to slip into the gap by discreetly placing his leg against one of the man's sprawling limbs and pushing against the knee. The leg itself neither resisted nor gave way, but the knee swung loosely off to one side. It was up to him, it seemed, to take the flaps of the yellow jacket that were draped over the seat and move them aside so he could sit down. He was expecting to be scowled at and cursed, shouted at and shaken off, grabbed by the shoulders and shoved away, but the man made no effort either to slide along the seat or to fight this character who had muscled his way in and was now so close to him. There was actually something creepier about being ignored so totally. To his surprise it was the passenger in the suit, who was still flopped forward, who twitched himself further off to one side. Spotting his opportunity, he piloted his upper body into the space between the two men and leaned back. Squeezed though he was between a rock and a hard place, he gave a sigh of satisfaction.

Things were looking up. Normally, like a dog after doing its business and kicking earth over it, he stopped caring about how his bets with himself turned out the instant they were over, but on this occasion he could feel the triumph and relief crawling up his spine.

This approach—dealing with problems as they came up—was definitely the right one. Cramped though he was, he managed a little nod of self-affirmation. No doubt about it. The cut on his nose, the hole in his trousers, the glasses nearly falling off—he had successfully contrived a complete reversal of the morning's run of bad luck.

From somewhere came a sharp, disconcerting crack. It was a sound like a dry thing splitting and breaking. After a pause long enough to make him think it had stopped, it started again. It happened so regularly that he felt it had probably been going on for quite a while before he noticed it.

Craning his neck, he peered around to see where the

181

noise was coming from. Past the door to his left, through the standing passengers, he spotted a man sitting reading a newspaper. The man held the paper rigidly vertical, presumably so as not to intrude on his neighbors' space. His face, hidden behind dark glasses and a surgical mask, was hard to make out, but a sharp crack could be heard at regular intervals after he had finished turning a page. He couldn't be sure if the man was rapping the edge of it with the back of his fingers, or if the paper itself was screaming at being pulled so tight, but one thing he could sense clearly in the paper's distractingly harsh reaction was the man's bottled-up anger.

The train came to a station and the doors opened and closed. More passengers got on than got off and the place started getting crowded. He could no longer see the newspaper, but the sound reached his ears even more distinctly. The fellow was plainly just turning the pages, not actually reading. This rapping of his had plainly gone on well past the number of pages—thirty? forty?—the morning paper probably contained.

He had been feeling elated since squeezing himself into the little space on the special seats, but he could sense his good mood wilting as the repetitive sound got on his nerves. When he absentmindedly touched the side of his nose he felt a twinge of pain and the pad of his finger was a shiny red. He had changed his trousers, so there was no hole in them, but the discovery of two brown stains on one leg was depressing.

His predictions were no use with things like this. They came not simply because he wanted them to, but spontaneously. Nothing was going to happen when he was just sitting there, having to listen to an irritating noise. His bets imposed themselves on him before he had time to think, and his predictions spoke to him before he knew his own feelings. So, at times when he was not confronted with any

182

choices, all he could do was keep a low profile, staying alert to his surroundings to make sure nothing bad happened to him.

Suddenly the man in the jacket pushed up against him, with one arm tensed and his body swiveling so he could see outside. The train slowed down. It was evidently about to stop at the next station. Having checked whatever it was he wanted to know, he swung back around, elbowing him away, and began jiggling his spread legs up and down directly alongside. If the fellow intended to behave as though he didn't exist, he decided, then he would do the same in return, but just when his leg was about to start mimicking the quivering against its flank, he braced his toes and pressed his foot to the floor.

By now the train was sliding along the platform. The door beside him opened and passengers streamed out in large numbers. He felt the thick yellow arm beside him jerk as his neighbor, who had been staring vacantly at them, suddenly stiffened.

—What the fuck? barked the man in the jacket, leaping violently to his feet and blundering out onto the platform, pushing a path through the passengers who were getting on.

Free at last, he felt as if a heavy rock had suddenly rolled off him, and felt the emptiness that went with it. In a flash he slid across from the middle seat to the one beside it. The end seat was not only comfier, but he'd noticed a shiny object lying on the edge of it that he could hide by sitting on top of it. While there was something unsavory about the way the fabric was still warm with the heat of the leg-jiggler, he was far more concerned about whether anyone else had noticed whatever it was that had been left behind. He held his breath as he waited for the doors to shut. When a plump old woman ensconced herself in the now empty middle seat, he pressed his thighs hard against the partition from which a metal pole

183

rose. He was worried about Yellow Jacket realizing and rushing back. He only began to relax when the train gave a spasm and started to slowly move off. He breathed the air around him deep into his lungs. Its tang had changed; now there was a dull, dark brown smell, familiar and evocative, drifting about. He remembered. It was like the Chinese medicinal drink his granny used to take. His body relaxed.

Pretending to grope for his pocket, he slowly moved his left hand down his side. Passing the partition without stopping, his fingertips came into contact with something hard in a little heap in between the edge of the seat and the partition. It made a muffled clinking. He looked up and around but all he saw above him was the bored-looking face of the straphangers staring out of the window and a fat back propped against the partition beside him.

Sliding his hand away from his thigh, he brought it back out in front, where he stealthily opened his fingers and looked inside. On his hand sat three keys attached to a silver key ring. He guessed that the long one was a door key and the short, flat one a car key, but he had no idea what the other key, which was thin and light, could be for. The things I have in my palm control the greater part of the day-to-day life of that hulking character in his egg-yolk yellow jacket. He cheered up immediately. With this precious find safely in his possession, he shut his eyes and abandoned himself to the motion of the train.

When he reached his station, he descended the stairs from the platform and emerged through the ticket barrier, still not decided what to do with the keys. He knew that he was unlikely to hand them over to the station Lost and Found, but that didn't mean he wanted to take them back home with him either. The keys were a foreign object that felt unexpectedly heavy at the bottom of his pocket.

The oppressive white hospital building of over twenty

184

stories was visible further along the street he took from the station. He pictured a patient with a cut on his nose going through the automatic door and producing his appointment form and hospital ID card at the outpatient desk.

That was when it came to him. What if he threw the keys away? He needed an unusual amount of luck, so a high-stakes bet was in order. As if under compulsion, he found his legs taking him toward a sturdy arch-shaped bridge spanning the river, which would soon run into the sea. The wide road led straight there. Leaning on the stone parapet, which came up to his chest, he waited for any passersby to move off, then quickly withdrew his hand from his pocket and spread his fingers wide. The bunch of tangled keys plummeted, dwindling in size and disappearing into the muddy river without a splash. He felt as though he had fallen with them. As he beat a hasty retreat, he heard his grandma's muffled voice:

—You'll be punished for this.

Her words expanded inside him like ripples in water.

—Don't worry about it. It means my checkup will turn out okay.

He had thought he was getting rid of something but ended up with this now clinging to him.

—You'll be punished, repeated the voice. He saw the pale bloodstain on the fingers he had touched his nose with.

—I'll deal with that when it happens.

He gave an exaggerated wave of his hand and went into the hospital.

185

IN REVERSE

Though it was the end of November, the day was distinctly sunny. In the vicinity of the house, however, it wasn't mild or still enough to be described as an Indian summer and a cold, biting wind blew in when he opened the window on the north side a crack. Nonetheless, the thermometer in the sun-drenched living room had registered over 20°C before noon.

Kyusuke Hoda thought of their house as being divided into two parts. Go to the north-facing windows and you could hear the autumn wind even when they were shut; cross over to the French windows which faced south and you were bathed in sunlight that prickled and burned the skin. Where exactly is the north-south demarcation line in this place, he wondered, edging his way over the parquet floor from the French windows to those on the north side. It was only a small room, but he managed to find a spot where his left shoulder was cold while his right side was nice and warm. On the wall in front of him was a clock. The minute hand had just gone through the warm half of the face and was now starting its climb through the cold zone. The hour hand had dragged itself a good way through the chill air and was now approaching the apex. If the movement of the hands was influenced by their being on the way up or down then the temperature difference between the two sides of the clock face probably threw things very slightly out as well, he thought. But it didn't take him long to realize that since the

189

hands moved in a circle, left and right would balance each other out even if that were the case.

—What are you doing standing there?

The sudden opening of the French windows and the sound of Sasako's voice startled him. In a black varsity jacket over a red sweater, she was standing on the terrace rubbing her forehead with the back of her grubby gardening-gloved hands.

—Must be cold out there.

—You're supposed to be going to Dr. Kumano's today. It'll be lunchtime soon if you don't get a move on.

—The afternoon'll be fine. He always has lots of patients to see in the morning.

—What's the point in doing what you did last year, having the test but not going to get the results?

—Look who's talking.

—That's not true. This year I went two weeks later. I admit last year it took me six months.

—It just makes you feel a bit better for a little while.

Mulling over what had happened the previous year—he'd forgotten all about it until she had brought it up—Kyusuke smiled wryly as he left the hot-cold dividing line to move over to the south-side windows. Since the health checkup for senior citizens that the local government sent them notice of every autumn was free, they always went to the Kumano Clinic nearby, but they tended to feel things were over and done with once they'd had the X-rays and blood tests; going to get the results seemed too much of a hassle, and they let time pass. I wonder if Dr. Kumano gets checkups too, thought Kyusuke irrelevantly while gazing at Sasako's rounded back in its varsity jacket as she stepped down into the garden again from the narrow terrace. The logo of their daughter's university stood out, white on black. He watched her walk off holding a trowel in one of her gloved hands

190

until she soon vanished behind a mimosa bush.

The wind from the north didn't slacken in the afternoon.

—You are going to go, aren't you? When Sasako pressed him a second time, he finally dragged himself to his feet and put on his thick half-length coat.

—You'll need a hat. Going out into the cold suddenly is a good way to burst a blood vessel. Her commentary pursued him all the way to the front door like a spoken guarantee.

—Especially if you've not got a lot of hair, he added as he obediently put a woolly hat on his head and opened the door.

The moment he left the perimeter of the house and emerged onto the street, the north wind swept over him. When he turned at the street corner and set his face for the Kumano Clinic, a headwind met him full on and instinctively he turned up the collar of his coat and drew his head down into his shoulders. The wind groaned and rumbled at the foot of the sky and the dead leaves scuttled by his feet. Wonder if this qualifies as a real "tree blaster," he was thinking as walked on, chin pressed against his chest as if to cut a path through the wind with his woolly hat. He remembered having heard of a tree blaster level 1. Could this be level 2 or level 3, and even stronger? A bicycle which had overtaken him came to a standstill a little way ahead, and the woman on it put her feet down, turned her back to the wind, and gave a little shriek.

—I can't keep going.

The wind blew her exasperated voice to Kyusuke's ears as he got closer. She was a middle-aged woman with a small, pale face and rimless glasses, but her lips, like a little flower in bloom, were the one thing he could see with complete clarity in the wind.

—It's dangerous. You should get off and push.

191

His warning came out spontaneously. The woman gave a brisk nod, dismounted, rearranged her grip on the handlebars, and started walking alongside him. She had a white plastic supermarket bag in the basket at the front of the bike, with the transparent corner of a package containing what looked like a piece of clothing protruding from just under the loop.

—Have you been shopping? Kyusuke asked, worried she might not manage to stay upright.

The woman reeled, bicycle and all, when a block of wind smacked into her, and she gave the same cry again.

—I can't keep going.

—Just take it slowly and it'll be okay. We're right in the path of the wind.

At some point Kyusuke grabbed the narrow luggage rack at the back of the bike and begun to push. The woman seemed grateful and, with this impetus from behind, started to move forward with uncertain steps. Apparently she said something to him, but the wind ripped her words to shreds and blew them away so he heard nothing. He pushed the luggage rack with greater force by way of reply. There was a lull in the wind and the bicycle suddenly shot forward.

—Hey! he heard her cry out, dismay mingling with a little laugh as the handlebars dragged her skipping along.

But the games the wind played with them only lasted until they got to the clinic further down the street. Stopping, Kyusuke tried to pull the bicycle to a halt. The woman, noticing a change in their progress, turned and looked at Kyusuke quizzically.

—I'm going in here, he said, pointing at the signboard and nodding good-bye.

—Oh, you were going to the hospital. I'm so sorry.

As the collar of her wine-red coat flapped in the wind, he saw a look of misgiving behind her glasses.

192

—It's just a checkup. To see if I'm alive or not. You take care now.

—You'll be fine. You're obviously in good health. Good luck with the checkup.

Almost losing her footing in the gusting wind, the woman stood as firmly as she could and gave him a stiff little bow from the neck.

When he opened the door and went into the waiting room, the air was muggy, with an alien, cellar-like smell very different to the outside. Kyusuke recognized a hint of pharmaceutical pungency in it as he announced the purpose of his visit to a woman at reception whose face he knew, then removed his woolly hat and lowered himself onto the long bench. Because it was the afternoon or due to the strong wind, there were not many people waiting—just a mother with two young children and an old lady. As Kyusuke adjusted to the stagnant air of the room lit by fluorescent ceiling lights, he felt sweat starting to form on his forehead. Was it just his imagination or were his heartbeat and his pulse a little faster than usual? It was annoying to think he'd come all this way only for Dr. Kumano to find his blood pressure higher than normal. If he asks me why, I'll play the geriatric card and put it down to the strong wind and the temperature difference from outdoors. He remembered the old doctor once telling him that some people's blood pressure shot up at the mere sight of the white coats of the hospital staff. "I can't keep going." The little shriek the woman gave with every gust of wind came back to him.

For some time Kyusuke heard the sound of a child crying on the far side of the door before he was summoned into the consulting room in its place. There was a bigger window than in the waiting room and although the blinds partially blocked the rays of the afternoon sun, the room felt as bright as if he had just climbed up from a cellar. The florid-faced doctor contemplated the medical file he was holding for some time, arranged two similar-looking documents on his desk, confirmed his name—Mr. Hoda?—then went silent.

—I'm here for the results of my recent checkup.

Dr. Kumano's silence made him feel uneasy and he craned forward on his stool as though pulled toward him.

The doctor finally spoke. He looked up and faced his patient.

—I wonder if you're taking any medicine right now?

—Not really. Except for vitamins . . .

The doctor, who had two or three long hairs sticking up out of his eyebrows, nodded silently and cocked his head to one side.

—Is there something wrong with me? asked Kyusuke in a whisper.

—Wrong . . . well . . .

—Which bit of me?

—Can't really pin it down to a specific place.

—Is it something to do with aging?

—You exercise?

—Walking and not much else.

—Wonder if people used to like walking as much as they seem to now.

I think the fellow's deliberately rambling on to avoid having to say something difficult. Suspicion only fanned his anxiety.

—Like my granddad. After he retired, he spent all his time looking after his bonsai trees and playing go.

Without meaning to, Kyusuke played along.

—That's the previous Dr. Kumano, right?

—His was the right way to live. Anything else and . . . well . . .

The irritation he felt toward this fellow, who kept shaking his head as he shuffled the papers around his desk with

194

his fingertips, intensified. He felt a pang of doubt; surely the man's passed the age when he can function properly as a doctor.

—So, Doctor, what can you tell me about the results?

—The thing is, Mr. Hoda, you are not getting any older.

—So you're saying there's nothing wrong with me?

—That's what's wrong with you.

—Being unable to get any older?

—I can't be sure until I've had more time to observe its progress, but looking back over the last two or three years makes me think you may have Retroannuation Syndrome.

—Retroannuation?

He felt a rush of anxiety at the unfamiliar term.

—Going backwards in age.

—Is that an illness?

—Since it's the opposite of aging, I suppose it's unnatural.

—I'm getting younger?

—It's not necessarily a good thing.

—You mean, because cancer would progress faster—that sort of thing?

—And that's not all, I'm sure.

—What would you advise me to do?

—It's the same as getting older; there's nothing the medical profession can do.

Thrusting the test results toward him, the doctor spun his chair around and turned his back to him. The body language was clear: this consultation is over. Goodbye. The expressionless voice of the nurse telling him to take care reached his confused mind.

—I don't understand. I don't think I'm doing anything out of the ordinary . . . he muttered plaintively, reeling from the alarming information he'd had thrown at him as he got up from the stool.

195

—It's nothing to worry about. Recently I've had the occasional patient like you.

—And are they all okay?

—One of them was killed in a car crash the other day.

With a sense that a strange kind of logic was at work there, he left the consulting room. There wasn't a single patient in the waiting room outside. If I'd known the doctor had this much time, I'd have pushed for more details, he thought regretfully. "You take good care of yourself now," said the receptionist in a singsong voice, sticking her face through the little window in the wall. It'd be nice if he could just stop getting older. Trouble was, how far would the getting younger go? Thinking of the future, he began to feel shaky, like someone standing on the edge of a big black hole. He was conscious of a weight on his back as he pushed open the front door of the clinic.

There was no one on the dusty residential street down which the wind still gusted, and the only sound was the rattling of autumn leaves in the sun. The sensation of pushing the bicycle came back to him as vividly as the weight of a woman's body. Maybe it was the bizarre condition he'd just been informed about that had made him so keen to help, he reflected, and he sunk his head into his collar, as though he were being watched. Making up his mind not to tell Sasako the results of his checkup, he pulled his hat down closer to his eyes. The wind, which had been blowing right at him a while ago, had turned into a tailwind and was pushing him from behind. Kyusuke headed home more or less at a run.

Even when they got into December, it was still a warm winter. The temperature fluctuated but no wave of intense cold came, and over the weeks he could check the progress of the season by studying the way the sun extended gradually deeper into the house through the window. The dividing

196

line between hot and cold crept off the face of the clock and moved, he guessed, more to the north. The misgivings provoked by Dr. Kumano's diagnosis gradually faded over time. When he went out for a walk he would stumble on the irregular surface of the sidewalk; he had to grab the handrail when his legs proved unwilling at the station stairs; if he got up for a pee at night, getting back to sleep wasn't easy. It hadn't been like that when he was young. Nowadays you heard the word "aging" all over the place, but "retroannuation" was something he'd never encountered before. Sometimes he felt a twinge of suspicion: maybe that doctor had just been pulling his leg.

He spent the winter solstice lounging in a bath with some yuzu in it that Sasako had bought, and when the boxes of special New Year's dishes he'd ordered at a department store were delivered and it was time to welcome in the New Year, the air was chilly and crisp and winter had really settled in.

He got the news of the death of a former colleague about two weeks into the new year on an overcast and bitterly cold day.

—Urushihara is dead, he heard Tsutsuno tell him in a gloomy voice on the phone.

—But he was fine in autumn, Kyusuke protested. Urushihara had been organizing their get-togethers since the first one to mark fifty years since they had all joined the firm.

—That, apparently, was the problem.

—That he was well? he asked, holding his breath.

Tsutsuno didn't reply to this, but told him the time and place of the wake and the funeral, adding: —I'm planning to go, but it's cold, so you shouldn't go unless you want to.

Urushihara, who had been appointed president of a subsidiary company just before reaching statutory retirement age and had stayed in the position for an unusually long time

197

before calling it quits, had the loudest voice of anyone in their group and showed no outward signs of decay.

—I won't go to the wake, but I will go to the funeral as it's in the daytime, said Kyusuke before putting the phone down. "He was a bit young to die," Tsutsuno's murmured comment lingered. They'd joined the firm in the same year, but the real sorrow lay in losing a friend with whom he'd spent time getting room and board at a company dormitory attached to one of the company's factories in the provinces.

The temple Tsutsuno had specified was near a station on a line that served the suburbs. It was a small concrete building with an eccentrically round roof. It looked so drab that if the land spreading out behind it had not been packed with gravestones and wooden grave tablets, he would have had trouble deciding whether this treeless enclave was a temple or not. The congregation was small and the only face that Kyusuke recognized apart from Tsutsuno was Katayama, another member of their group. The voice chanting sutras went quiet as they finished the offering of incense, and everybody got ready to leave after paying their respects to a little gray-haired lady, presumably the wife of the deceased.

—Shall we go with him, see him on his way? asked Tsutsuno, indicating the hearse parked on the road in front.

—Let's watch from here. That'd be better, answered Katayama, his voice muffled behind a white mask he had taken out of his pocket. Why here would be better Kyusuke had no idea, but he quickly assented.

The three of them began walking toward the station through the afternoon chill which felt as though it would probably end up snowing if it started to rain. He didn't think he had come from a sense of duty, but the funeral had been so modest and quiet that he'd had trouble getting into the swing of it, and a guilty sense of inadequacy nagged at him inside.

Kyusuke didn't realize he had walked on ahead and left

198

the other two behind until he heard Tsutsuno's voice behind him.

—Hey, you're going too fast.

—Do you always walk like that? said Katayama damply inside his mask, looking astonished when he caught up.

—You don't act your age, unlike us, Tsutsuno slipped in ironically.

—He must be the same age as us. We all moved into the company dorm at the same time.

—Yes, but different people age differently, declared Tsutsuno, who was now walking alongside him.

—It's not a matter of not being able to. Just that lately I've completely lost any desire to walk fast, mumbled Katayama, the tallest and longest-legged of the three.

—That makes sense. Urushihara may have jumped the gun a bit, but we're growing old gracefully enough.

Am I included in that "we" of Tsutsuno's? worried Kyusuke.

They went into a coffee shop near the station to get out of the cold and away from the heavy, cloud-smothered sky, but their conversation was listless and kept tailing off.

—I heard he was playing golf into this year, Tsutsuno said. His tone suggested it was something he'd just remembered.

—Yes, when we got together last year, he said he was playing a couple of times a week, Katayama chimed in, gazing dreamily out of the window.

—If he had made it to eighty, then he might even have got round the course in fewer shots than his own age.

—That's certainly what he was hoping, agreed Katayama before the conversation tailed off again.

—How've you been lately? Tsutsuno turned to Kyusuke, who'd been sipping his coffee in silence.

—Fine, I guess. Never been much of a golfer, though.

—But you look so well, said Katayama with authority,

grinning and sounding thoroughly insincere. Jealousy Kyusuke could have handled, but the sense of being a bit of a freak got on his nerves.

—Look at you. You've got a good color, you can walk fast—I think you may actually have gotten younger than last time we met in the autumn, said Tsutsuno, clearly poking good-natured fun at him.

—Maybe you're right.

Kyusuke guessed that it would be over with faster if he played along and didn't argue.

—Getting younger at our age is no easy matter, murmured Katayama, with a theatrical sigh.

In response, Tsutsuno suddenly became quite talkative.

—Wasn't there a story about that? I can't remember if it was a folk tale or one of Aesop's fables, but there's an old fellow who begs the gods to make him young again. His wish is granted and he keeps getting younger and younger until he ends up a baby.

Without wanting to, Kyusuke jumped in with an objection. —That's impossible. Even if you do get younger, your bone structure isn't going to change, so there's no way you can go all the way back to babyhood.

His tone was quite intense, brittle. The other two stared at him.

—Once your adult teeth have come through, the size of your jaw is fixed. It can't change . . . If you could grow a second set of baby teeth, well, that would be a different story.

—Yes, that would be overdoing things, said Tsutsuno in a conciliatory tone, waving his hand deprecatingly.

—I wonder what sort of age one can realistically go back to, Katayama continued, blithely oblivious of Tsutsuno's attempts to calm things down.

—Your twenties at the most, I would guess, answered Kyusuke. He looked abstracted, thinking of youth

200

and beyond.

—Urgh. You really want to go through that again?

—Not me. I'm happy to go on getting old, as nature intended, Tsutsuno announced to no one in particular as he tried again to put a lid on the topic.

—But can you be sure you'll age in the right way? Kyusuke asked him. His eyes now seemed to have the whole stretch of age in mind.

—I'm already way past the three score years and ten measure of life.

—We've still got our seventy-seventh, eightieth, and eighty-eighth to go. Lots of lucky birthdays . . . Katayama rambled on absentmindedly.

—So let's all go quietly off home.

After tipping his already empty coffee cup to his lips one final time, Tsutsuno got to his feet. He paid the bill with a five-thousand-yen note, and the other two gave him a few hundred-yen coins each, then propelled him out of the place while he grumbled about not having the right change for them.

They were in sight of the station and heading toward it when Katayama suddenly stopped, held his hands out in front of him, palm upwards, and looked up at the sky. Something cold floated down and touched the nape of Kyusuke's neck.

—You know, Urushihara . . . Tsutsuno had begun to say, when the alarm on the level crossing started ringing to announce the approach of a train.

—No hurry, no hurry, the other two said, stopping Kyusuke, whose instinct was to make a run for it.

—It's too cold to wait at the station, he replied, as if to excuse himself, but he didn't really feel like abandoning his friends and running to the ticket machines by himself anyway.

Katayama smiled benignly and gave a little jerk of his chin in his direction.

—You old people are so damned impatient.

There was the odd day when snow fell halfheartedly or mornings when the garden was covered in frost, but by and large the long-term forecast was right and winter that year was warm. There were even nights when he would end up in a mild sweat in his down futon after setting the dial of the radiator a bit high. Kyusuke was in the habit of getting up once a night to go for a pee. Late one night he felt the urge to urinate and found himself shuttling to and fro across the boundary between dream and waking.

Hearing a soft, murmuring voice in the darkness, he managed to extract himself from a baffling dream in which something—what exactly he couldn't tell—was seriously amiss, and listened carefully, his head on the pillow. The murmur thickened, changed into a kind of a groan and then a high-pitched shriek just as he was about to ask his wife what was wrong. It sounded as though she had said "Damn fool," but there was more fear than complaint in her voice.

—Wake up. You're having a bad dream.

Kyusuke sat up in his futon, reached out to Sasako, and shook her. She must have been holding her breath, because she exhaled in a great gasp and spoke in a thick, muzzy voice.

—The egg broke.

—What egg was that?

—There were so many weird people there. We've got to protect Anne, I thought.

—Maybe you should leave that to her husband.

—When things get tough, you can't depend on that man.

She had finally broken out of her dream and her voice was becoming clearer.

—Like me?

—You? You're even worse.

—Even when I was their age?

—It's nothing to do with age.

Sasako went silent. With his head back on the pillow again, he could soon hear the mild breathing of someone asleep. Age has nothing to do with it; some people are just hopeless. Kyusuke saw the sense in that as he stood up to go to the bathroom. He heard a little laugh—cheerful, almost girlish—in the darkness behind him, and looked back.

—What?

—Try and dig some more . . . Look at it all.

Kyusuke went out, listening to the soft voice coming from the dark bedroom. The dim glow in the little window must be from a far-off streetlight.

Feeling more relaxed after he had finished his business, it occurred to him that he could just stay up. He knew that if he went back to bed it would take him a while to get back to sleep, and for once he felt like doing something a bit different. It was cold just in his pajamas, but he was confident he'd find something he could put on in the living room. When he switched on the light in there, the place appeared unusually stern and forbidding, though he had every reason to be familiar with it. The wall clock was at a little past three. An hour to go till the paper was delivered. He turned on the heating and pulled the day blanket that was on the sofa over his shoulders. With nothing to do, he went to the sink and slowly drank a cup of water. Sighing audibly, he switched off the light and the heating, and retreated to the bedroom.

—What's wrong?

Sasako was awake and her voice came from deep in the darkness.

—I went to the loo. Then I wandered round the house a bit.

—You could catch your death. Plenty of people collapse in the loo in wintertime.

203

—That's why I came back quite soon.

—I need to go too.

Her remark made him wait as he was about to shut the door.

—It's after three.

A warm shadow slipped past him and vanished in the direction of the bathroom.

Spring arrived early as though drawn in the wake of the warm winter. The rays of sun shining into the living room drew back bit by bit and there were more days when the heater wasn't needed in the bright middle of the day. Sasako announced that she would plant the spring bulbs earlier than usual and got very busy with her gardening. Their garden wasn't big, and with so many pots and planters jostling for space, the overflow spread to the veranda. He never managed to get a satisfactory answer when he asked about the names and colors of the flowers, but as happened every year, Sasako would acquire some new gardening books, which she pored over for hours, then went and bought all sorts of bulbs and seedlings before heading outside, trowel in hand and a look of serenity on her face, unlike when she was in the house. Kyusuke, who never felt like getting his hands dirty working with the soil, would just watch, sometimes wondering when she had become such a keen gardener. It wasn't that long ago; she had really thrown herself into it only over the last few years, after getting old. How long would she be able to keep it up?

—Feel like giving me a hand?

Kyusuke gave a start when she unexpectedly called out to him. Even her voice had a more cheerful lilt to it than usual.

—What do you want me to do? he replied noncommittally as, propelled by a vague sense of guilt, he pushed his feet

204

into a pair of sandals on the veranda.

—I want to bring those three planters over here where it's sunny.

He was about to grab the edge of a long, narrow container filled with fresh earth when she exclaimed:

—Not by yourself. You'll hurt your back. I'll take the other side, okay?

With a quiet "One, two, three," the weight of earth left the ground.

—Are they always this bad?

—When they're really heavy, I just drag them.

—You shouldn't. I mean, if you did yourself an injury, then who would take care of all this?

—That's the reason I'm careful.

Contemplating the planter they'd moved with a look of satisfaction, Sasako issued a rapid series of orders as if it had given a boost to her morale. The round terracotta pots went from beneath the eaves of the house to a spot where the rain could reach them; in their place went the Seto ceramic pot containing some Queen of the Night which had died but then sprouted again from the roots; some pansies, which had simply been dumped on the ground after she returned from the shop, were planted in a hole they dug by the front door; and a variety of herbs were installed under the mimosa. Sasako didn't look put out even when he asked if it really was the right season for transplanting things, and after a while she told this very occasional helper in the garden to go and change into some proper shoes, put on a new set of cotton gloves she produced, and help her with whatever jobs sprang to mind.

When she finally straightened up and surveyed the garden with a look that said, There, that's the preparations for spring taken care of, Kyusuke realized he was covered in a thin film of sweat from the unaccustomed work. It wasn't that he minded doing a bit of exercise, but the sensation of his damp undershirt clinging to his chest and back was unpleasant.

It was just too much trouble, so he made the mistake of ignoring her advice and not changing his underwear. In the bath he took before going to bed he soaked in hot water right up to his neck but he still felt a chill running up his back and along the outsides of his arms. When he got up in the morning his head ached, so without letting Sasako see he stuck a thermometer under his arm; it said 37.6°C.

After breakfast, he felt the shivers coming back again. Folding up the paper he had begun to read he got up off the sofa.

—I think I've caught a cold. I'll nip over to Dr. Kumano's and pick up something for it.

Sasako looked at him with a frown.

—It's unusual for you to say that yourself. Got a temperature?

—Not really.

—Maybe working in the garden yesterday wasn't such a good idea.

—Maybe. Or it could have nothing to do with that.

—They say pneumonia is very dangerous for old people. Dress up warmly and get going right away, she told him, with a glance at the clock as though checking that the clinic was open.

The faintly overcast sky was high and awash with light, and though there was little wind, there was a chill in the air that stabbed at the skin. Cramming his hands into his coat pockets, Kyusuke reflected that he almost never went to see Dr. Kumano on his own initiative, something he hadn't realized until Sasako pointed it out. He walked fast from the desire to have the doctor check on something else in addition to his cold. Every jarring step he took seemed to reverberate

206

dully in his head, but it never occurred to him to change his pace.

Whether because the flu was going around or because of the time of day, the waiting room seats were packed with people. Kyusuke handed his registration card to the receptionist and stood by the bench with a sigh. The consulting room door didn't open for quite some time, but after a plump old woman with a slight curve in her back and a cane emerged, all the subsequent appointments seemed to advance smoothly and Kyusuke managed to secure a seat at the end of the bench.

When the front door opened hesitantly and the timid figure of a woman appeared, Kyusuke, like the rest of the patients on the bench, barely gave her a glance. After presenting herself at the reception desk, the woman, who was wearing a pale beige coat, turned to face the waiting room. The eyes behind the rimless glasses swam around the room before coming to an abrupt stop on Kyusuke. The vivid crimson lips in the middle of her small white face seemed to move slightly. Her eyes passed on, though spontaneously he had started getting to his feet, and drifted over to the space left by a man who had stood up in response to his name being called, where she finally sat down. They didn't return to Kyusuke. She was without a doubt the woman whose bike he had helped to push the day the wind had been so strong. "I can't keep going"—the cry that had come from her small red mouth revived deep inside him and he wanted to walk over and have a chat, but he was too shy to do so in the cramped waiting room where everyone could listen in. She took a weekly magazine down from the shelf beside her, placed it on the folded coat on her lap, and turned the pages in a self-conscious way. Still looking at her, Kyusuke couldn't help feeling rather awkward.

His name was called and he went into the consulting

room. Dr. Kumano was seated in front of his desk, showing his profile, just like the last time.

—What seems to be the problem, Mr. Hoda?

The old doctor gently put the medical records he was holding down on his desk and swung around in his chair to face him. When Kyusuke said he had a temperature and the shivers, the doctor got him to open his mouth and inspected the back of his throat, palpated both sides beneath his jaw, and pulled down the skin beneath his eyes.

—Looks like the start of a cold, he said simply. Want to check your blood pressure before you go? he added as an afterthought. While Kyusuke rolled up his sleeve and stuck out his arm, he revealed the other reason for his visit.

—Retroannuation, you say? Last autumn?

—When I came to get the results of my checkup last year, you said I might have Retroannuation Syndrome.

—Do you feel there's anything not quite right with you?

—I'm not really competent to judge . . .

Dr. Kumano gave a ponderous nod, applied his stethoscope to Kyusuke's arm, and was silent for a little while.

—124 over 71. Good.

—Thank you. Is that the result of reverse aging too?

—You sound worried.

—When I think about the future, yes, I'm worried.

—Meaning?

—What'll I do when everyone I know gets older and I get left behind? Things like that . . .

—There'll be an endless supply of young people bubbling up from below.

—Maybe so, but the fact is, I'm an old man. Worse than that, I'm going to end up an old man who isn't really old at all.

—That's what characterizes reverse aging.

Detaching the stethoscope from around his neck the doctor

208

placed it on his desk and his florid face twisted into a smile.

—If the condition progresses, I'll be blooming out of season, won't I?

—I can't give you a definitive answer due to lack of data, but I have no reason to say no.

—Last time I was here, you talked about how your grandfather tending his bonsai trees was an example of what old people used to be like. English-style gardening's become quite popular lately. Do you think it might help?

—Strikes me as a bit less dignified, but still, nature's nature whichever way you slice it.

The doctor's indifference was clear from his tone and it was difficult to pursue the matter further.

—You don't suffer from the same condition, do you, Doctor? said Kyusuke, feeling an urge to hit back, as he rose from his stool.

—I'm past all that. There's no one to take my place, so I'm planning to shut the clinic down at the end of the year.

Kyusuke found himself staring back at Dr. Kumano's face. I see. You've got everything planned. The proper response failed to come to his lips.

—If I have any problems before then, I'll come back for your advice, he said and left the room.

—Take care of yourself now, the old doctor intoned cheerily.

Out in the waiting room, the woman whose bicycle he had pushed on that windy day was sitting all alone. Ms. Shimogawara. Her name was called. She stood up and their eyes met. The hint of an embarrassed smile flitted across her lips as she came face to face with Kyusuke, who gave a modest bow. They passed one other and he watched from behind as the figure in the pale blue cardigan passed through the door at the end of the room. I'll wait here till she comes back out, thought Kyusuke. He fancied walking along the street

209

with his hand pressed against the back of her coat rather than the back of her bike. But wouldn't that take me in the opposite direction to my place? His temperature may have risen a little, because he could feel a throbbing pulse in his already painful temples. He hoped that working out his bill and preparing his medication would take longer than usual so he would have less time to wait for her. He felt nervous and miserable at the thought that this clinic might be shut the next time he wanted to talk to someone about some change he'd noticed in himself. Behind the door, the consulting room was sunk in silence and not a sound emerged.

YOZO'S EVENING

The platform clock said seven minutes past ten when he got off the train.

Regurgitated from the heated coaches into the chilly air of the suburban station, the passengers trudged in silence toward the stairs of the bridge that led over to the ticket gates. Swathed though they were in coats and jackets of different colors, at some point the people swarming past him and funneling into the stairs' mouth seemed somehow to metamorphose into a single mass of dark backs. That's the color of going home, thought Yozo.

He turned his attention away from the stream of commuters and back to the clock above their heads. Eh? He gave a little gasp of surprise. He'd always thought that the clock, which was suspended from a beam above the platform, was black and round, but what now confronted him was something square, shiny, and green. The clocks in stations had had round faces with black hands creeping around them ever since he'd started taking the train to school sixty years ago. They had no business changing now. They're not like the wall clock we have at home. You don't need to wind them up. They're electric so they never go fast or slow. That was what his older brother had told him when they kids, and Yozo still believed that all the clocks in all the National Railway stations in Japan were all that same model and all ticking merrily away. So firm was this conviction that it had survived the privatization of the national railways some twenty years

213

ago quite undented.

He suddenly felt as though he had been tricked all these years. On the platform, he'd just been checking what the time was, not checking the time-giver. He didn't know when the changeover happened, but it wasn't only the shape; he'd been swindled of the time as well, which had flowed with such a nice circular motion inside that old clock. The dismay and annoyance brought Yozo to a standstill. The fact that he hadn't even noticed the change until a moment ago meant being tricked in yet another way.

Everyone had left the platform. Turning up the collar of his coat and sinking his chin deep into his scarf, he started for the stairs, his limbs dragging heavily. He thought he heard something when he passed beneath the clock. Had it been one of those phlegmatic old round things, the sound of the long black hands carving out the minutes as they circled the white face might well have reached him. But this square green object was clearly a slick piece of equipment that would never make so primitive a sound. I'm just imagining things, Yozo muttered to himself, pressing on. As he took hold of the cold handrail and placed a foot on the stairs he wondered at what point his own back darkened.

He had mounted the stairs left foot first again. You should always start climbing the stairs from your better foot, he'd been told by a former colleague whom he'd met after an interval of God knows how long at a get-together for retirees of his old firm. Get that wrong and you'll notice that things don't feel quite right on the way up. If that happens, you should go back down and start again from the proper foot. The man, who had made his case with bizarre intensity though his expression suggested he knew it was all rather far-fetched, had moved somewhere far away by the time the next retirees' meeting came around. He had brought up the subject when the two of them were going up the stairs at the

214

station on their way home after the event. Maybe even then the clock on the platform had changed from a chunky round one to the new square green model, Yozo thought with a lingering sense of regret as he placed his left foot on the first step after the small landing.

He got his breath back as he made his way to the exit along the passage, empty now that the swarm of people had moved on. He went through the ticket gate, which snatched and gobbled the ticket from his hand, carefully descended the stairs left foot first, and encountered a red light at the pedestrian crossing. A few people stood on the curb looking impatiently up at the light. There weren't many cars, but a set of headlights would suddenly come barreling up from one direction or the other if you ignored the red and tried to cross. Perhaps cars took precedence over pedestrians at night-time, but the lights showed no sign of changing. Instinctively reaching inside his coat, his hand pulled a pack of cigarettes out of his jacket pocket. He was about to light the cigarette he'd stuck in his mouth when he heard a voice from a short distance away and off to one side.

—Cut that out, grandpa.

Startled, Yozo looked up and saw a man in a windbreaker propped against a railing by the sidewalk. He automatically hid the hand with the lighter deep in his coat pocket.

Haven't lit it yet. Swallowing down the words that had sprung to his lips, he took a good look at the owner of the voice. It was a young man with a wan little face and short hair who was leaning there, one leg planted on the ground, a little way apart from the people waiting for the light to change.

—Bet you chuck the stubs wherever you goddamn please. It's immoral.

No, I don't throw the stubs in the street. After I put them out, I always keep them and take them home. Once again he

215

couldn't bring himself to answer back. "Immoral," the word tossed at him by the man, lodged itself deep in his mind in an unpleasant way. It wasn't so much that he was annoyed at being criticized, it just felt downright weird for a person like that to have used a word like "immoral."

Are you telling me I should follow the rules about considerate smoking printed inside the lid of the box? No, you can't be calling my attention to the dangers of secondhand smoke and the fact that some people can't stand the smell of the things. He was quite unable to shoot back any kind of reply.

The unlit cigarette still in his lips, Yozo turned away from the youth and waited intently for the light to change to green.

—What the fuck do you think you're doing, looking so damn smug.

The sharp voice seemed to cut into his cheeks exposed above his coat collar. It was some mercy that the other people waiting for the light all pretended not to notice, though they must have heard.

—Oi! Can't you fucking hear what I'm saying?

The man's voice was getting louder and angrier, but he stayed perched against the railing. If he comes up to me, I'll have to answer back or run away, I suppose, but maybe the fuss he's making goes with the area, the way a dog barks to protect its own patch. Still, the way he just keeps glaring at me without moving a muscle is creepy.

The light changed to green. After the long wait, the pedestrians surged eagerly across. I need to get in among them and slip around a corner on the far side of the road, thought Yozo, keeping himself as upright as possible so he wouldn't appear to be running as he strode across the stripes of the pedestrian crossing.

—Oi! Where'd you think you're going?

He hadn't yet made it to the other side of the street when he heard the voice from unexpectedly close. The man must have pulled himself away from the railing and cut across onto the pedestrian crossing. Yozo had the feeling that hurrying on ahead would be the best thing to do, and without even a backward glance he turned at the corner where a pachinko parlor was and headed for a street with, he hoped, a few more passersby. Walking near the station with a shouting man in tow might not look good, but the fear of not knowing what might happen to him in a dark and empty street was stronger. More than any fear of violence, it was the psychological state of a man prepared to use the word "immoral" that alarmed him. He imagined he could see through to the brittle bone structure underlying the small, pale face.

Passing an overlit fast-food joint and under the eaves of an amusement arcade he turned down an alley that led past the back of a bank. When he got level with a greengrocer's with the front shutter down, he could see directly ahead another street that ran through a stretch of bars and restaurants, with figures talking loudly and laughing outside.

If I can break away and make it through to the street with all those people, the guy will probably get bored and give up. He was panting out the hot air that filled his lungs when the man's voice, which he hadn't heard for a little while now, abruptly came at him from behind.

—What's the hurry, grandpa?

While there were passersby around he must have restrained himself, but the comment burst from him in the little stretch of dim side streets. The calculation Yozo sensed in this made him more scared than before.

—I'm going home.

The answer was automatic; it took him a moment to realize that this was the first time he had responded to the man. He had meant to keep ignoring him, pretending not to hear.

He panicked at the realization that talking back had brought the rupture between them out into the open.

—And what's so important about home?

—The wife's waiting.

—Bullshit.

The word sounded like a dry, rasping intake of misdrawn breath.

The two of them were now almost shoulder-to-shoulder as they went into a comparatively bright street. Yozo had a slight height advantage.

—Bet you're smoking now 'cos your old lady gives you hell if you do it at home, right?

The man spat this out like a gob of phlegm while a lively group making for the station passed them the other way.

—Even if I smoke, I never drop the stubs on the street. I take them home with me.

Out came the words he had suppressed while waiting at the pedestrian crossing.

—That ain't what I'm fucking talking about.

Suddenly the man's rasping voice was furious and Yozo could feel that the people walking by were turning to look back at them. Alarmed by the way his tone had switched from tamped-down to angry, he decided to keep his mouth shut. He crushed the unlit cigarette he held clasped in his fist inside his coat pocket.

The two of them kept on past the block of bars and clubs in silence. Ignoring the pitches of the touts in their bow ties and black coats and the come-ons of the women with cold-looking legs beneath their fur-collared coats, the two of them walked in brisk lockstep as though they had some business to attend to. The hope of shaking the man off simply by ignoring him had vanished from Yozo's mind. Now all he cared about was finding the opportunity to get away from him.

—This way, is it? The house where your old lady's

waiting? asked the man suspiciously when they emerged onto the main road and Yozo was about to cross. The shops along both sides of the lamp-lit thoroughfare all had their shutters down and there were quiet intervals with no cars. Not bothering to reply to the man's inquiry, he crossed the road and started down the gentle hill on the far side that led to a big intersection with winking traffic lights. This route home from the station would take him quite far out of his way, but he didn't feel like explaining himself. Revolving inside his head was one thought: I want to stop this character who's attached himself to me from getting anywhere near my house. The fear of sudden violence had weakened; instead he was oppressed by the idea of being followed around like this forever and ever, world without end.

When he reached the lights at the big intersection, he made a right in silence. He was getting further and further away from home. He was also walking faster than he normally did and his breath came fast while his chest felt hot.

—You *sure* it's this way?

The man was still following him, but had fallen a bit behind. The note of doubt was stronger now.

—I told you. It's a long way back to my place.

Yozo's reply was curt and cold. The uncertainty he detected in the man's voice made him feel he had the upper hand for the first time.

—So why don't you take the bus?

—Walking's healthy.

—Even though you fucking smoke?

—All the more reason.

They passed a pet clinic with darkened windows, a vending machine glowing brightly, a tiny playground with a swing and a slide. Yozo kept going, with the man, who had shut up, in attendance. He didn't have anywhere specific in mind; he just didn't want to let him know the location of his house.

219

But the way the street they were on seemed to melt into the darkness ahead made him uneasy. Even if he managed to shake him off somewhere along the way, it was going to be a very long and lonely walk home.

It was after skirting a parking lot with a wire fence and arriving at an intersection with a newspaper delivery center and an osteopath's that Yozo decided he had to bring things to a head sooner rather than later. He had to engineer a parting of the ways; he couldn't keep walking all night, and in a virtually deserted street giving this creep the slip was impossible. Inside the leather shoes he occasionally wore on outings his swollen feet ached, and his lower back was numb and tired.

—So where's your house?

Yozo had stopped. He made an effort to control his tone of voice.

—None of your bloody business.

He scrutinized the man's sulky face under the streetlights. It had something bird-like about it. One of his swollen-lidded eyes was a bit smaller than the other, and the blob of a nose beneath was a bungled-looking job. His dry lips were cracked, and a metal ring glinted in his left earlobe.

—I've had enough of this. Come on, you go home too.

He had begun to think that, were he asked, he would be quite happy to apologize for trying to smoke near the station earlier.

—What's that supposed to mean?

The tone was confrontational, but there was less force to it than before.

—Look, we can all get things wrong. For years I had the wrong idea about the station clock, for example. The damn thing's square.

—So?

—Not just that. The clock face is green, and the hands

220

are pale green too.

—What the fuck are you on about?

—I don't know myself. Why don't we both call it a day?

—And go where?

—Home. Where else?

—And where's that?

—Over there.

He casually raised his right arm as if to swat the whole thing away. It was only when the man turned to see where his hand was pointing that Yozo remembered what was actually in that direction.

—The housing estate?

—That's right. The housing estate.

His answer was immediate.

—They're gonna demolish it. Got your eviction notice yet?

—You're very well-informed.

—You're taking the piss. The place is empty.

—A few of us are still left. There's a while to go till the cutoff date.

Half what he said was improvised, but half was based on rumors he had heard. The estate had been built about fifty years ago on the former site of a military facility, but the buildings had started to deteriorate rapidly in recent years. It must have been a few years back that he'd learned it was due to be demolished. It was a long way from his own house so he had no idea what sort of condition it would be in now, but back in his sixties, when he was newly retired, he used to walk over to the avenue of cherry trees that ran through the estate in the springtime.

—So you're sticking it out there.

—Uh-huh.

Yozo gave a nod. He almost began to believe that he really did live in a decrepit, elevatorless apartment block that was slated for demolition.

221

—I'm off. Bye.

Yozo turned and, with a wave, stalked away toward the street lined with cherry trees in a manner that clearly said he meant it. Though it seemed unlikely he'd shake him off, the sudden absence of anyone close by brought not relief but unease, as if he were out there floating alone on the sea at night. He couldn't help looking back, to see a solitary, fidgety figure standing beneath a streetlight at the intersection gazing around him. A dry cleaner; a tofu maker; a bakery; a sweet shop—out of breath as he passed a string of shops that were a lot more modest than those near the station, a hope began to form inside him. I should be able to leave the guy behind if I make a sudden turn into an alleyway. But I need to put more space between us to do that—

—What's the hurry?

He had just spotted what looked like a narrow alley past a barbershop a little way ahead, when the rasping voice addressed him from behind. It was closer than he would have expected and he instinctively slowed his pace.

—You again?

His reaction was equal parts sigh and mumble.

—Not happy to see me?

The man overtook him, with both hands stuffed into the pockets of his black windbreaker, as though he were taking charge.

—I'm going to go on by myself. Leave me alone.

—Just forget about me.

—And you keep following me?

—Why not?

—It's like stalking.

—So? What's wrong with that?

—What'll you do when I go inside?

The man didn't answer; he seemed to slow down slightly.

—What'll you do when I shut the door and lock it

222

behind me?

—That what you're gonna do?

—It's my house. What else do you expect?

—Pfff . . . The sound he made could either have been a snort or a sign that he might be giving up.

—That's what I'm going to do, Yozo repeated. In his mind's eye he saw him as he'd been a couple of minutes before, standing alone at the crossroads under the streetlight looking around him.

—Do whatever you damn want.

He had a sudden, vivid image of the man staring at the closed door for a while before shrugging his shoulders and going off down the stairs.

The road had become a gentle slope that climbed beneath the cherry trees whose scrawny, leafless branches met overhead. From halfway up the hill, a succession of long rectangular buildings stretched back at ninety degrees on both sides of the road, seeming to float in the light of the tall mercury lamps. He hadn't been to the estate for a long time; in the night the buildings hunkered, dark and silent.

Past a bus stop with an overhanging roof stood a glowing public phone box and a broad road that cut across the estate from one side to the other, intersecting the avenue of cherry trees.

—Now which way? the man asked peevishly. Yozo said nothing and pointed left. A slightly sunken parking lot stood empty with faded white lines punctuating its surface; a single grimy car was parked in one corner.

As Yozo walked on, he realized that not one of the windows in the apartments on the higher piece of land was lit up and that they were cordoned off behind a wire fence with "No Entry" signs along the road. Many of the buildings on the lower side were also dark, but he could see some where the odd landing here and there on the common stairway was

223

lit. While the bicycle racks in front of the abandoned blocks were empty, in the few blocks where the lights were still on the presence of a handful of bicycles and tricycles made itself felt in the darkness.

Yozo's progress up to this point had been completely arbitrary so he was savoring the sense of safety that came from knowing there were still people living there. He also felt oddly pleased to discover that the story he'd come up with on the spur of the moment had become manifest fact.

After they had gone past several blocks the man turned to look at Yozo in exasperation.

—Now what?

Yozo jerked his chin perfunctorily: —It's a bit further on.

—So damn far.

—If you don't like it, you're free to go.

The man shrugged bad-temperedly but walked on in silence. Having come this far, Yozo now had no idea what to do. The fact that a few holdouts were living here was a godsend, but it was going to be tough to find a convincing destination somewhere in this half-ruined estate. The unanticipated nighttime walk had made his legs stiff and tense, and with the fatigue stretching from his lower back all the way to his calves, he moved sluggishly. Even if he managed to break away from this guy, he wasn't sure he'd be able to make it all the way home.

If they kept advancing through the estate they'd eventually reach the road that ran around the perimeter. The headlights of cars were visible now and then through the gaps in the bushes behind the last couple of blocks.

—We're gonna come out the other side, the man shouted as if the idea were intolerable.

—It's one further along.

In desperation Yozo pointed just beyond the block they were walking past, where a gentle incline led to another row

224

of similar-looking buildings. Noticing that the light on the open-air landing of the top floor of one of the buildings was on, he pointed up at it without a second thought. He had no idea if anyone was living up there or not, but he had no choice: he was drawn to the light like an insect.

With a glance at the number 19 painted in black on the cover of the fluorescent light by the entrance, Yozo gave an exaggerated little sigh.

—Here we are.

—What floor are you? asked the man, mistrustfully inspecting the building.

—Four.

The fellow took a couple of steps back and looked up at the light.

—You're lying, he whispered in a tone that was different from before.

—Come up and see for yourself, replied Yozo coolly. He didn't imagine that his saying this would actually make the man go away; it was just that he'd been driven into a dead end where there was nothing else he could do. Along with it was a vague feeling of incipient relief at having finally made it.

—I'm off then. Goodnight, he said, the civil sendoff coming out quite naturally.

Yozo went into the building, leaving the man standing there nervously rolling his shoulders. Cold, dank air enveloped him. The first step, on which he consciously placed his left foot, was higher than he expected.

When he got to the first landing, he saw someone coming up after him. It wasn't unexpected, but nor was it foreseen. His mind a blank, focused only on his feet, he trod punctiliously on each individual step. Gradually his breath got shorter. As he started running out of breath his lungs began to burn.

When he got to the third-floor landing, Yozo grasped the

225

cold ironwork and did some stretches for his lower back. The landing was dimly lit by the mercury lamp that stood at the corner of the block opposite. His panting breaths showed white.

He was about to mount the next flight of steps when from above he heard the dull thud of something heavy closing. Startled, he held his breath; the faint sound of footsteps—perhaps someone shuffling along without lifting their feet—reached his ears. He couldn't see anyone, but a gentle, dried-up sound drifted down to him.

—Why, good evening.

A small figure that had appeared beside the blank wall at the top of the stairs greeted him placidly.

—Evening. Here I am. Back at last.

He was winging it, but the words he came up with sounded pleasantly familiar nonetheless.

—You must have been cold. Tonight's a cold one.

Descending with a hand on the wall and carefully placing both feet on each step, an old woman stood before him, doing up her white coat.

—Where are you off to at this time of night?

—The convenience store over the road. Forgot to buy the yogurt for breakfast.

—Want me to go instead?

—No. I'm fine.

She seemed to be smiling in the faint light of the far-off lamp. On the landing Yozo watched in silence as the gray head, leaning into the wall, made its way very slowly down the stairs. She ought to have bumped into the young man about halfway down, but her precise little footsteps were the only sound that reached him. Behind one of the doors on the fourth floor, he guessed that there was a futon still warm from the woman's body heat. Bet she was only wearing pajamas beneath her coat. Yozo just stood on the landing, able

226

neither to go up nor down.

When the faint sound of shoes dragging finally ceased, the building sank into a deep silence.

—Back home are you, then?

He heard the man's voice from somewhere out in the night.

—How the hell do I know? Yozo flung back.

His hand groped inside his coat, grabbed the pack of cigarettes, and pulled it out. The flame of the lighter flared for a moment on the landing, then went out.

AFTERWORD

When the editor of a literary magazine approached me about writing a short story, I accepted without too much serious thought. The deadline seemed sufficiently remote and I wasn't working on anything very difficult at the time.

I had no idea what to write about, just a vague notion that something about thirty or forty Japanese manuscript pages long would probably be in order. The deadline did not require me to get down to work straightaway and I saw my short story standing proudly like a distant tower beyond all the other fussy little jobs I was working on.

Days, then weeks, slipped surreptitiously by and, before I knew it, the deadline loomed. I was alarmed to discover myself suddenly standing at the foot of a tower I'd thought to be far away. For several days, I wavered between thinking "You're not going to make it" and "You're still all right." During this period of alternating panic and nonchalance I somehow managed to read large numbers of totally irrelevant books. The blockage persisted. I still had no idea of what to write about.

But one day, like a drowning man clutching at straws, I seized hold of something: the ordinary, the routine, the everyday.

This book is the result of putting together twelve pieces all of which were created through similar acrobatics on an emotional tightrope over a decade. For better or worse, these short stories represent ten years of my life, from my mid-sixties to my mid-seventies.

Senji Kuroi
December 2005

SENJI KUROI is the penname of Shunjiro Osabe, a novelist from Tokyo who graduated in economics from Tokyo University. He worked as a "salaryman" while writing novels and was an Akutagawa Ryunosuke Prize candidate in 1968. The following year he published *Jikan* (Time) and in 2001 won the Tanizaki Jun'ichiro Prize for his novel *Life in the Cul-de-Sac*, which is available in English translation. He also has won the Yomiuri Prize and the Noma Prize and currently serves as president of the Japan Writer's Association as well as a member of the selection committee for the Akutagawa Prize.

GILES MURRAY was born in London in 1966. After graduating from the University of St. Andrews in Scotland, he moved to Tokyo to study Japanese. Among his translations are Kumiko Kakehashi's *So Sad to Fall in Battle*, Masahiko Fujiwara's *The Dignity of the Nation*, and Yo Hemmi's *Gush*.

SELECTED DALKEY ARCHIVE TITLES

MICHAL AJVAZ, *The Golden Age.*
 The Other City.
PIERRE ALBERT-BIROT, *Grabinoulor.*
YUZ ALESHKOVSKY, *Kangaroo.*
FELIPE ALFAU, *Chromos.*
 Locos.
IVAN ÂNGELO, *The Celebration.*
 The Tower of Glass.
ANTÓNIO LOBO ANTUNES, *Knowledge of Hell.*
 The Splendor of Portugal.
ALAIN ARIAS-MISSON, *Theatre of Incest.*
JOHN ASHBERY AND JAMES SCHUYLER,
 A Nest of Ninnies.
ROBERT ASHLEY, *Perfect Lives.*
GABRIELA AVIGUR-ROTEM, *Heatwave*
 and Crazy Birds.
DJUNA BARNES, *Ladies Almanack.*
 Ryder.
JOHN BARTH, *LETTERS.*
 Sabbatical.
DONALD BARTHELME, *The King.*
 Paradise.
SVETISLAV BASARA, *Chinese Letter.*
MIQUEL BAUÇÀ, *The Siege in the Room.*
RENÉ BELLETTO, *Dying.*
MAREK BIEŃCZYK, *Transparency.*
ANDREI BITOV, *Pushkin House.*
ANDREJ BLATNIK, *You Do Understand.*
LOUIS PAUL BOON, *Chapel Road.*
 My Little War.
 Summer in Termuren.
ROGER BOYLAN, *Killoyle.*
IGNÁCIO DE LOYOLA BRANDÃO,
 Anonymous Celebrity.
 Zero.
BONNIE BREMSER, *Troia: Mexican Memoirs.*
CHRISTINE BROOKE-ROSE, *Amalgamemnon.*
BRIGID BROPHY, *In Transit.*
GERALD L. BRUNS, *Modern Poetry and*
 the Idea of Language.
GABRIELLE BURTON, *Heartbreak Hotel.*
MICHEL BUTOR, *Degrees.*
 Mobile.
G. CABRERA INFANTE, *Infante's Inferno.*
 Three Trapped Tigers.
JULIETA CAMPOS,
 The Fear of Losing Eurydice.
ANNE CARSON, *Eros the Bittersweet.*
ORLY CASTEL-BLOOM, *Dolly City.*
LOUIS-FERDINAND CÉLINE, *Castle to Castle.*
 Conversations with Professor Y.
 London Bridge.
 Normance.
 North.
 Rigadoon.
MARIE CHAIX, *The Laurels of Lake Constance.*
HUGO CHARTERIS, *The Tide Is Right.*
ERIC CHEVILLARD, *Demolishing Nisard.*
MARC CHOLODENKO, *Mordechai Schamz.*
JOSHUA COHEN, *Witz.*
EMILY HOLMES COLEMAN, *The Shutter*
 of Snow.
ROBERT COOVER, *A Night at the Movies.*
STANLEY CRAWFORD, *Log of the S.S. The*
 Mrs Unguentine.
 Some Instructions to My Wife.
RENÉ CREVEL, *Putting My Foot in It.*
RALPH CUSACK, *Cadenza.*
NICHOLAS DELBANCO, *The Count of Concord.*
 Sherbrookes.
NIGEL DENNIS, *Cards of Identity.*

PETER DIMOCK, *A Short Rhetoric for*
 Leaving the Family.
ARIEL DORFMAN, *Konfidenz.*
COLEMAN DOWELL,
 Island People.
 Too Much Flesh and Jabez.
ARKADII DRAGOMOSHCHENKO, *Dust.*
RIKKI DUCORNET, *The Complete*
 Butcher's Tales.
 The Fountains of Neptune.
 The Jade Cabinet.
 Phosphor in Dreamland.
WILLIAM EASTLAKE, *The Bamboo Bed.*
 Castle Keep.
 Lyric of the Circle Heart.
JEAN ECHENOZ, *Chopin's Move.*
STANLEY ELKIN, *A Bad Man.*
 Criers and Kibitzers, Kibitzers
 and Criers.
 The Dick Gibson Show.
 The Franchiser.
 The Living End.
 Mrs. Ted Bliss.
FRANÇOIS EMMANUEL, *Invitation to a*
 Voyage.
SALVADOR ESPRIU, *Ariadne in the*
 Grotesque Labyrinth.
LESLIE A. FIEDLER, *Love and Death in*
 the American Novel.
JUAN FILLOY, *Op Oloop.*
ANDY FITCH, *Pop Poetics.*
GUSTAVE FLAUBERT, *Bouvard and Pécuchet.*
KASS FLEISHER, *Talking out of School.*
FORD MADOX FORD,
 The March of Literature.
JON FOSSE, *Aliss at the Fire.*
 Melancholy.
MAX FRISCH, *I'm Not Stiller.*
 Man in the Holocene.
CARLOS FUENTES, *Christopher Unborn.*
 Distant Relations.
 Terra Nostra.
 Where the Air Is Clear.
TAKEHIKO FUKUNAGA, *Flowers of Grass.*
WILLIAM GADDIS, *J R.*
 The Recognitions.
JANICE GALLOWAY, *Foreign Parts.*
 The Trick Is to Keep Breathing.
WILLIAM H. GASS, *Cartesian Sonata*
 and Other Novellas.
 Finding a Form.
 A Temple of Texts.
 The Tunnel.
 Willie Masters' Lonesome Wife.
GÉRARD GAVARRY, *Hoppla! 1 2 3.*
ETIENNE GILSON,
 The Arts of the Beautiful.
 Forms and Substances in the Arts.
C. S. GISCOMBE, *Giscome Road.*
 Here.
DOUGLAS GLOVER, *Bad News of the Heart.*
WITOLD GOMBROWICZ,
 A Kind of Testament.
PAULO EMÍLIO SALES GOMES, *P's Three*
 Women.
GEORGI GOSPODINOV, *Natural Novel.*
JUAN GOYTISOLO, *Count Julian.*
 Juan the Landless.
 Makbara.
 Marks of Identity.

FOR A FULL LIST OF PUBLICATIONS, VISIT:
www.dalkeyarchive.com

SELECTED DALKEY ARCHIVE TITLES

SELECTED DALKEY ARCHIVE TITLES

The Third Policeman.
CLAUDE OLLIER, *The Mise-en-Scène.*
Wert and the Life Without End.
GIOVANNI ORELLI, *Walaschek's Dream.*
PATRIK OUŘEDNÍK, *Europeana.*
The Opportune Moment, 1855.
BORIS PAHOR, *Necropolis.*
FERNANDO DEL PASO, *News from the Empire.*
Palinuro of Mexico.
ROBERT PINGET, *The Inquisitory.*
Mahu or The Material.
Trio.
MANUEL PUIG, *Betrayed by Rita Hayworth.*
The Buenos Aires Affair.
Heartbreak Tango.
RAYMOND QUENEAU, *The Last Days.*
Odile.
Pierrot Mon Ami.
Saint Glinglin.
ANN QUIN, *Berg.*
Passages.
Three.
Tripticks.
ISHMAEL REED, *The Free-Lance Pallbearers.*
The Last Days of Louisiana Red.
Ishmael Reed: The Plays.
Juice!
Reckless Eyeballing.
The Terrible Threes.
The Terrible Twos.
Yellow Back Radio Broke-Down.
JASIA REICHARDT, *15 Journeys Warsaw*
to London.
NOËLLE REVAZ, *With the Animals.*
JOÃO UBALDO RIBEIRO, *House of the*
Fortunate Buddhas.
JEAN RICARDOU, *Place Names.*
RAINER MARIA RILKE, *The Notebooks of*
Malte Laurids Brigge.
JULIÁN RÍOS, *The House of Ulysses.*
Larva: A Midsummer Night's Babel.
Poundemonium.
Procession of Shadows.
AUGUSTO ROA BASTOS, *I the Supreme.*
DANIËL ROBBERECHTS, *Arriving in Avignon.*
JEAN ROLIN, *The Explosion of the*
Radiator Hose.
OLIVIER ROLIN, *Hotel Crystal.*
ALIX CLEO ROUBAUD, *Alix's Journal.*
JACQUES ROUBAUD, *The Form of a*
City Changes Faster, Alas, Than
the Human Heart.
The Great Fire of London.
Hortense in Exile.
Hortense Is Abducted.
The Loop.
Mathematics:
The Plurality of Worlds of Lewis.
The Princess Hoppy.
Some Thing Black.
RAYMOND ROUSSEL, *Impressions of Africa.*
VEDRANA RUDAN, *Night.*
STIG SÆTERBAKKEN, *Siamese.*
Self Control.
LYDIE SALVAYRE, *The Company of Ghosts.*
The Lecture.
The Power of Flies.
LUIS RAFAEL SÁNCHEZ,
Macho Camacho's Beat.
SEVERO SARDUY, *Cobra & Maitreya.*

NATHALIE SARRAUTE,
Do You Hear Them?
Martereau.
The Planetarium.
ARNO SCHMIDT, *Collected Novellas.*
Collected Stories.
Nobodaddy's Children.
Two Novels.
ASAF SCHURR, *Motti.*
GAIL SCOTT, *My Paris.*
DAMION SEARLS, *What We Were Doing*
and Where We Were Going.
JUNE AKERS SEESE,
Is This What Other Women Feel Too?
What Waiting Really Means.
BERNARD SHARE, *Inish.*
Transit.
VIKTOR SHKLOVSKY, *Bowstring.*
Knight's Move.
A Sentimental Journey:
Memoirs 1917–1922.
Energy of Delusion: A Book on Plot.
Literature and Cinematography.
Theory of Prose.
Third Factory.
Zoo, or Letters Not about Love.
PIERRE SINIAC, *The Collaborators.*
KJERSTI A. SKOMSVOLD, *The Faster I Walk,*
the Smaller I Am.
JOSEF ŠKVORECKÝ, *The Engineer of*
Human Souls.
GILBERT SORRENTINO,
Aberration of Starlight.
Blue Pastoral.
Crystal Vision.
Imaginative Qualities of Actual
Things.
Mulligan Stew.
Pack of Lies.
Red the Fiend.
The Sky Changes.
Something Said.
Splendide-Hôtel.
Steelwork.
Under the Shadow.
W. M. SPACKMAN, *The Complete Fiction.*
ANDRZEJ STASIUK, *Dukla.*
Fado.
GERTRUDE STEIN, *The Making of Americans.*
A Novel of Thank You.
LARS SVENDSEN, *A Philosophy of Evil.*
PIOTR SZEWC, *Annihilation.*
GONÇALO M. TAVARES, *Jerusalem.*
Joseph Walser's Machine.
Learning to Pray in the Age of
Technique.
LUCIAN DAN TEODOROVICI,
Our Circus Presents . . .
NIKANOR TERATOLOGEN, *Assisted Living.*
STEFAN THEMERSON, *Hobson's Island.*
The Mystery of the Sardine.
Tom Harris.
TAEKO TOMIOKA, *Building Waves.*
JOHN TOOMEY, *Sleepwalker.*
JEAN-PHILIPPE TOUSSAINT, *The Bathroom.*
Camera.
Monsieur.
Reticence.
Running Away.
Self-Portrait Abroad.
Television.
The Truth about Marie.

FOR A FULL LIST OF PUBLICATIONS, VISIT:
www.dalkeyarchive.com